The Probate Killer AI wants you to Die.

Copyright © 2024 Michael O'Brien
All rights reserved.
ISBN 979834509795:

Dedication

I dedicate this book to my wife who inspired me to write it. I have written that sentiment five different ways and pondered the probabilities of what conclusions readers might make. I want to add something like; "Not that she wants me to kill or that I want to kill her…." Sadly, those who would think ill of the first sentence would probably use the second as proof that they were right. Fortunately, such ruminations are not necessary. When you have a healthy bond with your spouse you don't need to say much. If I dedicated the book to our dog she would still know who I am and how I feel. To my wife, she knows and deserves to know and that is all that matters.

Chapter One

Los Angeles, California is a sun bronzed lie. Whoever created the phrase "Tinsel Town" understood that a shinny lie was more believable than the truth. Marcos Alvarez didn't understand that. He had visited his Aunt, Rachel Haddon in the Los Angeles suburb of Monrovia California several times over the years but he never understood what life was like in "La La Land." He was stationed at the Army recruiting office in Oak Cliff, Texas with a little more than a year left in his service when Aunt Rachel died. Angry that he wasn't told in time to attend her funeral he called Richard W. Adler the lawyer handling her Probate.

"She was an amazing woman." Adler said "Very passionate. Her entire estate was going to Charity." That didn't make sense to Marcos. Not because he was told, more than once, that he would inherit her house but because charity was never that important to his Aunt. He needed a lawyer.

Jennie was late. She hated that. She had a new client at 9:00 and did not anticipate that the battery in her Ford Escape would be dead after two weeks in Mexico with Jack. For the first time in weeks she was dressed like a professional and it felt good.

Black skirt, flat no pleats. Soft wool, the kind that produced little fibers that floats on the air. Pleats made you look like a school girl destroying the professional look she worked hard to achieve. The skirt was precisely three inches below the knees. Lower then a school girl uniform but high enough not to look formal. Black nylons completed the look, hard to find in any color other than black or white. She never wore white stockings. "The days of women looking professional but still like a women are fading." She told friends but the truth is, they were already gone. She hated the synthetic pants suits women wore. Pants suits had become a "uniform" for professional woman but she did not want to look like she was trying to fit into a man's world.

Jennie idolized Dolly Parton, all business but still all Woman. She wanted to be the same way minus the boots unless she was going to a country dance. She never let her emotions control. Bitches got angry, business women were firm and firm was always better than angry. She clasped her necklace behind her neck on the first try.

Today's necklace was a single tear shaped polished onyx stone which worked with her high buttoned Coral colored silk blouse. She skipped Sapphire, Emerald and Pearls but considered the round Ruby. Pearls went with everything but she wore them a lot and wanted her first day back to be a little special. A quick glance and a smile in the mirror even though she already knew she looked right. Black jacket also wool but not matched to the skirt. She held it over an arm too hot to wear it anyway.

She hated that she had to call Jack for a ride to work so soon after they got back. It violated her fourth rule for dating: "Give the guy some alone time…especially after a long trip together." She debated calling an Uber but knew that if Jack found out it would be a slap in his face and that was worse. She jumped in gave him a quick kiss added "no rush." It was a worthless lie because Jack knew she hated to be late.

Jack pulled into the driveway and manually down-shifted the transmission of his black Dodge Challenger Hellcat producing an audible burp from the rear tires yanked down by the steroid infused Hemi. "Oops." He said as he swung into a spot. She knew he was lying.

"Oh, you don't have to stay. I have inconvenienced you enough." Jennie said. Thinking it was clear she meant "Go away, I have to work."

"Nonsense." Jack replied opening his door.

"Dewey Cheatham and Howe has the world's best coffee, and with what I paid you guys I should get a free cup." Jennie didn't mind Jack's joke name for her law firm or that he made fun of lawyers. The firm was small and they never advertized. Creating false expectations was nothing but trouble. She didn't like trouble. Slipping through the back door she did not have time to look at the mail or say hello to anyone before meeting with Marcos Alvarez her potential new client.

Marcos walked into her office with a brisk military gate just as she was catching her breath. He was wearing Ironed jeans and brown boots under a blue polo that had a small red stripes. He explained that his Aunt died in Los Angeles and that her lawyer told him he had not inherited anything because it was all left to charity. He was certain something was wrong. She couldn't have kids and he was her only nephew. She always told him he was going to inherit her house. "I even read the Will once." He said completing his pre-planned speech as he looked at her ready to hear what he wanted.

Jennie told him he needed a California lawyer but because she had just got back from a long vacation, or because he looked like he was a little lost, she let him ramble. Three times through the story was enough. She didn't cut him off because she knew how to handle people. She directed the conversation. California is what she needed him to understand, so she was sure to mention it four times.

She stood as she had many times before signaling that the meeting was over and walked to the side of her desk. Marcos stood because she had like she knew he would. She extended an arm to her office door and they began a slow walk.

"A properly signed Will can be challenged if it was procured by undue influence, but you need a California lawyer to do that."

Jack stood as if he was Jennie's next client when he saw Jennie and Marcos walking down the short hall to the lobby. Jack was still in "vacation mode," boot cut stonewash Levi's and a Grunt Wear t-shirt. A Xerox of what he wore the day before and pretty much every day. Jennie told him there was no such thing as "Boot cut Stonewash Levi's," they made Original fit, Stonewash jeans, Boot cut, Relaxed fit, Athletic fit, 517's, 501's, etc. it was a system.

"I didn't buy them that way." Jack answered "I had to stone wash them myself with Lava soap. I was going to call them volcanic jeans but Wrangler already trademarked that name." That was her boyfriend. A rambling jokester living for the minute and now, he was at her work.

"Maaam." Jack said drawing out the "a" so he sounded like a hick. "I need to sue Dunkin Donuts. I dunked one and only got half a donut back." Marcos laughed, Jennie suppressed a grimace.

"Marcos this is my boyfriend, Jack. Jack, this is Marcos Mendoza. Jack gave me a ride today because my car would not start." Jennie said professional as ever.

"You should hire her Marcos." Jack using a serious tone pointing to Jennie like they were in a bar.

"I mean, I am trusting her not only with the cost of the lost donut but the coffee too." Marcos smiled.

"Exactly." Jack continued as if Marcos had agreed. "That half donut went somewhere, and we all know there is only one place it could be, in the coffee. Their defective donut damaged my coffee! I'm not going to drink a donut. The donuts should take a dunking and stay in one piece. That's why they call it Dunkin Donuts. It's false advertizing for sure." Jack said looking at Jennie.

Jennie smiled thinking that an Uber would have avoided her being trapped in the "Breakfast at Tiffany's meets Easy Rider" moment in her office. Marcos smiled and said "I would, but I guess I need to get a California lawyer."

"Whoa, Commifornia, sorry to hear that." Jack said.

Marcos laughed and nodded.

"You can't do it?" Jack asked looking at Jennie, suddenly all business.

"No. Well I could get admitted Pro Hac Viche, but you're better off with a local lawyer, there will be a lot of Court appearances, and it doesn't make sense to fly back and forth." Jennie said not understanding that her response continued the client meeting she was trying to end.

"We could go to Cali for a while. It might be fun so long as you don't hack whatever it was you just said up somewhere." Jack said making a grimace.

Jennie rolled her eyes, forgetting she was in front of a client. "Pro Hac Vice," she said with perfect Latin enunciation. It means "For the Matter."

Jennie had already determined that Marcos probably didn't have a case. People can change their Will at any time. The law says no one has a right to inherit anything. Challenging a Will meant that you were picking a fight with the lawyer that drafted the Will and it was usually over before it began.

"Something is going on; my Aunt wouldn't have left her house to Charity." Marcos said "I have to find out."

Jennie looked at Jack and she could read his face. "It could take months." Immediately regretting that she said it because it opened a door she had already closed.

"Months of sitting on the beach, soaking up some rays learning to surf. Yeah, that would be brutal." Jack said with an easy smile.

"Jack." Jennie said more the impatient girlfriend than the prospective lawyer.

"Look" Jack said back to being serious. "I'm not saying fight to the death, but a few weeks that's probably all you need to get him an answer. If he has a great case get him somebody local, and if it's hopeless let him know so he doesn't spend years chasing nothing." Jack looked at Marcos. "One thing for sure, she will tell you straight good news or bad."

Marcos looked at Jennie. He could not tell how good she felt that Jack understood and respected her work. There was a short silence and that was all Jack needed to know that he had to pack, or rather not unpack from Mexico and get tickets to 'Lost Angeles.'

Chapter Two

Flying first class from Dallas to Los Angeles was two hours of luxury and free drinks that passed in the blink of drunken blood shot eyes. Tuesday was not a busy day for flights but first class still buffered the crowd. Jennie had filed the paper work to be admitted Pro Hatch Vice with an Objection to the Probate Petition and Counter Petition on behalf of Marcos Alvarez. The Court hearing was set for Thursday. Jack made sure he and Roger had suits so they would look like they belonged.

Roger never felt right in a suit. Blue jeans, square toe cowboy boots and beer was all anyone ever needed. Wearing flat front dress pants from Neiman Marcus made him nervous. The deep blue dress shirt and matching black jacket didn't relax him. They were comfortable but at more than $1,500 before tailoring, he was "too nervous to fart."

Jack shrugged off Rogers comment with a quick laugh as he slipped on a bespoke tan cashmere wool jacket over pleated black pants and a pressed white shirt with onyx cuff links and matching collar stud. Roger though Bespoke was British for "best" especially because he knew Jack had bought it on line from a London tailor using measurements he took with his phone.

Roger felt better after he slid into the driver's seat of the rented black Chevy Suburban. Black, what other color was there he thought as he scanned the electronics. "Top of the line. Works for me." he thought as he paired his phone. He used the navigation to get back to the terminal. He didn't really need it but the test was good and he would need it later. He wondered how anything got done in the jungle of humanity they called LAX. Jack and Jennie slid into the back seat after tipping the baggage handler who smiled at the amount as he loaded the bags into the back of the Suburban under Roger's stern gaze. He was on the job.

"9641 Sunset Boulevard Beverly Hills" Jack said. He didn't tell Jennie where they were going but got the smile he wanted from her as they pulled in.

"The Beverly Hills Hotel, baby." Jack said. "We're going first class Hollywood style."

Roger dropped them at the front door, and stared at the Valet through the window of the Suburban.

"It's Beverly Hills Roger; you're never going to find a spot to park, might as well let him." Jack said. Roger grunted and snapped the shift lever into park with a thump.

Jacked smiled looking at Jennie knowing his surprised worked. "Hamilton, two rooms." Jack said at reception. He reserved and paid for the rooms on line so there was little to do but sign for the keys.

"I have two keys to the Rodeo Bungalow Suite and the two keys to a Superior Room.' The part time model said with a "Hollywood smile" as she slide two sets of key cards far across the marble counter in a staggered manner making sure the big room keys were closest to Jack. It was a rehearsed move designed to show Jack respect. Jack slid the superior room keys to Roger.

"You might need two." Jennie was still smiling as he handed her a key card.

"Please have the bell man put our luggage in the rooms. "We are going to take a walk." Jack said, sliding two one hundred dollar bills across the desk.

"Yes sir" the girl said with a genuine smile.

"What are you doing?" Jennie asked.

"Rodeo drive." Jack said, "Surprised?"

"Can I get you the house car? It's complimentary." The hostess said.

"Sure." Jack said surprised. She walked around the counter like she was on The Price is Right but stopped after a few steps to make a sweeping gesture with her arm toward large doors outside of which was a black limousine. They piled into the car and not knowing exactly what to ask for, Jack simply said "Rodeo Drive please." The limo pulled out of the driveway and turned on Hartford Way proceeding straight onto Rodeo Drive.

The few blocks of palm lined Rodeo Drive was, by Beverly Hills standards, the poor part of town. The lots were too small for Mansions but typical tourists had no way of knowing that.

As the car rolled slowly into the business district Jack only recognize a few stores. Ralph Loren was a name he knew, but Lacoste, Vera Wang and Chanel were not brands that cared much about his Texas demographic. The limo driver went all the way to Wilshire so the tourists could see the golden triangle before he turned left to go up Beverly Drive. Jack finally recognized a familiar store, the Sunglass Hut and then the Cheesecake factory.

"Sunglass, we need those." Jack said asking the driver to stop. In typical Beverly Hills style the driver stopped in the middle of traffic not bothering to pull to the curb. The three of them got out of the limousine clutching the number to call for a ride back. They wandered for a bit and landed in a booth at the Cheesecake factory reading the same menu they had in Texas.

Chapter Three

"It's all the same." Roger said sliding into a familiar Cheesecake Factory booth like he did back home.

"No they're not. Some are handsome, some are skinny. They're all different." Jennie said.

"Not the guys, the food, and those guys are no different than Steve Smuckstein." Roger said.

"Steve Smuckstein?" Jack said with a laugh, figuring it was joke name.

"Everybody knows Steve Smuckstein" Roger said, using a sarcastic tone. "Total Romeo. All these guys bring their chicks here and try to impress them with how cool they are, how much money they have, how connected they are, bla bla bla. They have no idea what women want. " Roger said.

"And you do? " Jennie asked knowing Roger had plenty more to say.

"Of course. They want a man that can protect them." Roger said, as if he were the only one who ever thought of it.

"Doesn't money protect them? it feeds them." Jack offered pointing to the menu because he was paying.

"No, I mean caveman protect." Roger said.

"Caveman?" Jennie said making it a question. Jack looked at her with a "Wait for it expression,"

"Look,' Roger said. "This is something you probably don't even know about yourself Jen, All women have a primitive part deep in their brain."

Jennie tilted her head which she always did when she thought she was being conned. "I do love a harry chest." She said rubbing an open palm on Jacks shirt, mocking Roger.

"Now listen." Roger said continuing. "Why do women hate snakes? Why do women jump up on chairs when they see a mouse? Jennie shrugged her shoulders.

"It's the cavewoman part of their brain. Deep down in a part of the brain they don't know they have something says jump, and they do. That's the same primitive part of the brain where attraction lives." Roger said finishing about half of his lecture on the topic.

"Another round." Jack said looking up for the waitress as much to be funny as to actually get a new drink. Jennie smiled.

"And men, do they have primitive brains too?" Jennie asked in a mocking tone.

"Of course, why do you think sports are popular? Instead of hunting food we throw chase and kick balls, same thing, different decade." Roger said draining his beer. Roger had more to say. He always had more to say.

"If you took away electricity and banks we would all be living in caves." Roger paused for Jennie to say something positive like "okay," but not long enough for her to start the argument he knew she was working on.

"So Steve, he was always falling in love with these girls. Some girl would say hi bat her eyelashes and he was planning the wedding. I remember one time we were at the County Fair. Steve comes up to us and says Mary Jo what's her name has a crush on him."

"Mary Jo? At the County Fair? Jennie interrupted. "Was she wearing cut off jean short shorts?" poking at Roger.

"No, no, it's true." Roger said "I can see her in my mind. Dirty blonde, blue eyes, freckles but not too many just across the bridge of her tan little nose, whistle around her neck, dancing back and forth in her red one piece swimsuit."

"What?" Jennie asked. "At the county fair?" Interrupting Roger's embellished memory.

"Lifeguard." Roger said before Jennie could finish the question.

"No, just listen, listen. We called all the girls he was in love with "Mary Jo," making air quotes, because he was such a hick." Roger said.

"I got it." Jennie said to Jack, "Mary Jo, the cowgirl in her Daisy Dukes. Now it makes sense." Jack said.

"Steve wanted to be a farmer and he dreamed of the perfect girl, Mary Jo" Roger said making air quotes when he said Mary Jo. "He figured she would bring him lemonade as he sat on the tractor plowing the fields and then next to him on the big porch swing as the sun set."

"Sounds lovely." Jennie said poked fun like Jack did.

"So Steve is at the Fair just goin' on and on about this girl." Roger emphasized the word girl so they would quit poking at him about the name.

"So we tell him she likes ice cream and he gets this look." Roger laughed remembering how funny it was.

"Steve if you want to impress her you gotta take her an ice cream cone but it can't be just any cone. You gotta take her the best cone ever. Now Steve, he gets this looks in his eyes and man he is dreaming." Roger said enjoying the memory.

"Cone? Is that code?" Jennie asked. Making a double entendre neither of them understood.

"It can't be a double dipper, not even a triple. I said and he looks at me like I am some sort of genius. You gotta give her a cone she aint never seen before one that 'bout nobody has ever seen before, a double triple dipper. Now old Steve boy that guy was dumb in love with this girl just like all the girls that made the mistake of looking at him for more than two seconds. Sure enough, he said it like he was in church; A double triple dipper. That's right I said, and just think about how long it will take her to eat it?"

"Probably less time than it takes you to tell this story." Jack said interrupting Roger who ignored him and continued.

"So off we go to the ice cream man. Steve throws down his money and grabs the cone with one hand, and his in the other. He takes off walking slow and steady but he is too excited to maintain it.

"What color was it?" Jack asked. Just to annoy Roger.

"I don't know, just listen. He had all six stacked and I say don't forget the cherry on top. Everybody knows you have to have a cherry on top a double triple scooper."

"Nothing less." Jennie said poking like Jack did. Roger ignored her and continued.

"Hurry up I told him before it melts, so off he goes walking fast but the ice cream started to melt and the cherry started to slip off the top. So Steve starts hoofing it like ten miles an hour and he is pushing that cone side to side trying to slide the cherry back on the top." Roger demonstrated waving his arm back and forth.

"Then just as he gets there he pulls the cone hard to position the cherry and wham the top three scoops of ice cream fall off right onto Mary Jo. Oh man we laughed." Roger said smiling.

"Mary Jo was facing away from him and she turned her mouth was wide open. She was trying to figure out what happened. What the hell are you doing? She screamed at him. Probably the first time in her life she ever cussed, melted strawberry ice cream running down her hair.

Look what you did she yelled at Steve, scoop of vanilla sliding off her shoulder. Steve then tried to wipe the ice cream off, but the idiot was using the cone thinking he could somehow restack the scoops.

Finally Mary Jo swings her arm like she is trying to swat flies and the cone broke. Both of them were covered with melted ice cream then the girls run off to get washed up and Steve slinks back over to us. Dang, he said that was bad. But we were laughing too hard to say anything."

"That is your caveman story?" Jennie asked. "That's a terrible story."

"No it's hilarious." Roger said.

"You made a fool of your friend." Jennie said.

"No, no." Roger said dropping the tone of his voice as his laughter faded "He made a fool of himself. We told him a million times, to stop with wanting to marry women who glance at you, life isn't like that. We taught him a lesson and saved his ass."

"Some kind of lesson, what happened to him?" Jennie asked

"Ah," Roger sighed, his face suddenly blank washed with a sadness they could not understand.

"He joined the Army came home bought a crotch

rocket, dumb ass hit a tree." Rogers's eyes floated up and to the left. He did not know it but in that moment he was not able to look at them. Jack saw it and understood.

One thing we all share, pain comes in many forms and without invitation. Roger was no better at recognizing or dealing with it than anyone else. It snuck in when he wasn't ready.

"Nice ending Roger. I still think you made a fool of him." Jennie said.

"Nope he made a fool of himself; we all do, sooner or later." Roger said looking for a brief second into Jennie's eyes, and then left again into his own mind at his own failings. "Mostly because we lie to ourselves and then actually do things that only work in the lie." A moment of clarity he would have regretted if he was paying attention.

Jack was stunned. As much as Roger behaved like a "simple hick," somewhere deep down he knew what was important.

"Now that's a topic." Jack said staring square and straight into Roger's eyes as he sipped his drink inviting the deeper conversation he craved.

"Look around." Roger said in a serious tone that Jennie did not expect. "Do you think all these guys are being honest with their dates?" Roger looked at Jennie with a genuine look she didn't like.

"No." She said. "I wasn't born yesterday. I am sure some of them are lying to get what they want." Jennie said.

"No, they don't lie to get what they want; they lie to protect the relationship." Roger said.

"Because that's what they want." Jennie answered.

"Do I look good in this dress?" Roger said. "Yes dear; a lie to protect the marital relationship. Can you come over for dinner? Sorry we have a family birthday party. Lies to protect friendships."

"Men lie to get what they want in the moment." Jennie said.

"Women lie to look good." Roger commented wanting it to be a general observation.

"I don't lie like that." Jennie said.

"Really." Roger said, turning in his chair to look at her. 'Crap' Jack thought. He was afraid of Roger and Jennie squaring off. Jennie froze. She was having a good time and had not prepared herself for the possibility that her past would take a seat at the dinner.

"What lies?" Jennie said staring at Roger to see if he knew as an adrenaline kick caused her to unconsciously uncross her feet and shuffled them so her right foot was flat on the floor ready to take her weight if she decided to run.

"C'mon." Roger said, probing because he didn't know her that well. "You're telling me you have lived a lily white life of perfection. You never snaked a parking spot, never lied in Court, never stole a flower from the neighbor's garden. Is that that I'm looking at? Ms. Lilly White Jennie?"

Jennie was still tense. "Of course." She said annoyed because Roger sounded like he was speaking to a child.

"You never downloaded a song you didn't pay for. That's stealing Jennie." Roger said.

Jennie didn't respond. Jack could see that she was tense but didn't understand why. He was sitting to her left more than a foot away but he could feel her muscles strain. Time to step in, maybe past time he thought.

"We lie to protect ourselves from pain." They both stared at Jack. He could tell they were not drunk enough for that deep of a conversation but he continued.

"Lies protect you from being alone." Jack paused hoping they would think about the point he was making.

"That's life's ultimate pain." Jack said observing their expressions. He wanted to talk about what made people matter, what made life worth living. He usually avoided the topic because he was afraid they would reject his ideas, an irony that was not lost on him.

"Most people are naturally loners." Jennie said.

"I don't know about that." Roger said. "People are pack animals. They act like stupid sheep."

"Neurons that fire together, wire together." Jack said. They looked at him with blank faces. "Seatbelts." Jack said thinking they would connect the dots.

"What?" Roger asked.

"We put seat belts on without thinking. Our brains are wired to do it. We are not born sheep or loners, republicans or democrats, our brains get wired and once wired they repeat the same connections. Mental pathways turn into roads then freeways with very few exits. Think something long enough and you will not be able to think differently. Neurons that fire together wire together."

"Makes sense." Roger said. "I think I need a drink, I think I need a drink, I think I need…" Roger said his voice trailing as he repeated over their laughter.

"Life is about connections." Roger said, surprising Jack with a deeper thought than he expected.

"Speaking of which, with your permission I am going to see if I can connect with one of those girls at the bar." Roger stood up and grabbed his half full drink.

Jack nodded toward the bar. Roger didn't need to ask and they didn't need to talk. Roger knew that Jacks nod meant; "Don't do anything stupid."

"I like Roger; he has some deep thoughts for being the macho type." Jennie said as Roger walked away.

"He is interesting." Jack said keeping it simple because for the first time he suspected she was lying.

Chapter Four

The Los Angeles County Superior Court at 111 North Hill Street was a large old building the County built into a natural hillside stretching from Grand Avenue to Hill Street. The never ending population growth in Los Angeles gave root to additional Courthouses year after year. Unlike the green laminate in the Van Nuys Superior Court nicknamed the "Brady Bunch Court" before it was re-modeled, the Central Court had traditional non-descript wood paneled walls.

"Metal detectors?" Jack asked as they waited in line to get inside. "I should have thought of that." He added with a sad tone looking down at his brand new leather shoes which he neatly tied just an hour earlier.

"Boohoo" Jennie said with a smile. "Welcome to the world of paying a price to look good. A skill woman have been mastering for generations." She added with a little giggle. Jack looked at Jennies outfit for the first time. He only noticed women's fashions when there was a "problem," which meant when they fell off.

He told a friend in high school that he would probably get more girls if he learned to appreciate the effort woman took to look good, knowing the advice was for him too. He got wrapped up in making sure they were not late for court and forgot to tell Jennie how sexy she looked in her business clothes.

Jennie was wearing a black wool pants suit. They were all wool. The wool was probably mixed with another fabric but he had no idea what. It had no shine and as he put his hand in the small of her back he could feel how soft the fabric was. The pants were straight legs that tapered from the waist to the ankle maintaining the same one inch distance from her body regardless where you looked. "That's a hell of a trick" he thought.

Under the jacket Jennie was wearing a blue silk blouse. Jack knew the correct paint color for every Ford Mustang built in the 60's. He never caller one white he always said "Wimbledon White" because that is the name Ford gave them. "Caspian Blue" he thought as he glanced at the blouse but he didn't say it because it was a Mustang color. The blouse was periwinkle but Jack could never guess that. He only heard of periwinkle once and thought it was "some British guy."

Jennie never mentioned shoes. Jack suspected she spent more time picking her scarf then the simple low heel black leather shoes she always seemed to wear. The scarf was the thing and Jack knew it.

"Nice scarf. You look good." Jack said as they inched forward so Jennie could put her leather black bag on the belt of the x-ray machine.

"Thank you." Jennie said with a smile, laughing to herself about how long it took Jack to notice. The scarf was called "Plumes en Fete" in white, yellow and gray. It was one of Hermes finest.

Jack didn't need to know that she spent more time looking for scarves than it would take to fly to Paris and buy them.

The three found the courtroom with the help of a deputy and were early enough to get seats. They looked around but would not have been able to identify Richard Alder from any of the other tie wearing "hustlers" that wandered in and out. Jennie had taken a moment to step forward and speak with what Jack guessed was a clerk collecting business cards. The court was not loud, but the silence was noticeable when the Judge came out and took the bench to talk to the crowd.

She gave a little speech that Jack didn't really understand then everyone stood up and raised their right hand to take an oath. Jack and Roger stood up like everyone else but Jennie gave them a wave and they sat back down. Things moved quickly with lawyers stepping out of the crowd to talk with the Court then leaving or sitting back down.

"Estate of Rachel Haddon" the Judge finally called and Jennie walked to the tables inside a little railing. At five foot five attorney Adler was shorter than most. His jet black hair was perfect. It was dyed, but Jack did not pay attention. His grey flannel suit looked like it had just been pressed. He spoke to the Judge with Jennie. They were given a bunch of dates which they jotted down then turned to leave. Adler held the little door at the railing for Jennie then followed her back toward the doors the lead to the hallway. Jack glanced but did not get a good look at Adler. Roger and Jack followed them into the hall.

"Welcome to Los Angeles." Richard Adler said with a smile which looked normal to Roger and Jennie but Jack didn't buy it.

"I see you brought a crew." Adler said, "Who is on your team?" Jennie introduced them as her office something. Jack didn't pay much attention because he was stuck looking at Adler, more than just trying to figure him out, Jack was measuring him.

Adler was wearing a white shirt with a red tie that had a grey and mustard colored diamond print. He was wearing an old fashioned metal tie clip that held his tie to his shirt. "Military" Jack thought but Adler's hair was longer than a military cut parted on the right and jelled so it was perfect.

Black leather wing tip shoes. Kinda weird Jack thought were those classic or was Adler just odd.

Adler continued asking questions after the introduction he was controlling the conversation and that got Jack's attention. They talked about the hotel and Adler made some recommendations for sightseeing. Jack had difficulty not staring at Adler's brown eyes as he looked at each of them. Jack looked away only long enough to make sure Adler wouldn't know he was staring. "Nice meeting you" Adler finally said shaking Roger's hand then turning he squared his shoulders on Jack. "Nice meting you too Jack." he said looking Jack in the eye as he extended a hand ready to squeeze Jack's.

Jack shook, firmer than usual but he felt Adler's grip increase to be firmer than his all the while staring Jack in the eye corners of his mouth slightly turned up. Jack tried not to change his expression, but the slight downward tilt of his head and squint in his eyes was enough for Adler to win.

"That was quick." Roger said, turning as Adler walked away to face Jack and Jennie closing the circle.

"It usually is." Jennie said.

"Plenty of time to hit the beach." Roger added already dragging out his speech in a relaxed tone." They turned to look at Jack, who was watching Adler walk away.

"He killed her." Jack said.

"What?" Jennie shot back almost in a whisper.

"He killed her." Jack said, with a certainty. "I don't know why but he killed her."

"That's crazy." Jennie said.

"How do you know?" Roger asked indulging his

boss.

"I just do." Jack said. "Didn't you see the way he looked?"

"I didn't see anything." Roger offered, "Well other than another suit."

"No, not how he looked to us, how he looked at us." Jack said.

"What are you talking about?" Jennie asked.

"He didn't look at us." Jack tried to explain. "He didn't really look at us, he was measuring us, sizing us up."

"Typical lawyer, all hat and no cattle." Roger said, and then added "No offense." toward Jennie. Jennie paused trying to understand Rogers comment. She suppressed her desire to ask him why he uses odd ball phrases and to confront him about trying to look cool, because Jack's comment was crazy.

"That's not a killer." Jennie said. "Beside he wrote the Will and the only reason we are here is to attack it and by extension attack him. He has reason to be on edge."

"It was more than that. He controlled the conversation, he squeezed my hand to try and dominate me. It was a lot of things and let's not forget the change in the Will and all the money going to a charity no one has ever heard of."

"The Will was changed a year ago Jack." Jennie offered. "And it proves at best, that he stole from her not that he killed her. If he killed her it would have been a year ago when he changed the will."

"Na." Jack said, "Think about it. He makes money when people die. If business is bad what do you need?" Jack turned to look at them. He knew they knew the answer but he said it anyway. "You need people to die." Jack did not pause long enough for them to argue.

"You have a client, no real family it would be easy to change their Will and then, well 'end them' before they meet somebody who wants to romance the cash." Jack said.

"I think your losing it." Jennie offered. "Not only is that a terrible assessment of humans in general, but this guy." She said pointing down the hall where Adler had walked. "He has plenty of money."

"You never have enough money." Roger offered.

"There you go." Jack said nodding to Roger. "If we can figure out what the charity is we might know. I mean it's not the Red Cross or something people know about."

"Do you want me to birddog that?" Roger offered.

"I can find out who rented the PO Box, but it may not help us. I need a person and an address." Jennie added then continued. "They probably filed for a 501 C3 tax status but if your right that's all documented. We can get names for sure."

Jack was in a serious mood which Roger couldn't understand but it didn't matter he was ready to go to work.

"Roger, you got Adler's office address better go see what you can find out." Roger shrugged, he didn't need to understand. What Jack wanted was his mission. The beach could wait.

"You got it, as soon as I drop you guys off." Roger said.

Chapter Five

Roger sat in the black Chevy Suburban staring at Adler's office door. It had only been five minutes and he was remembering how boring stake outs were. That stiff feeling was already creeping back into his football knees. Thursday, a good day for a business stake out.

Roger had a theory that the world only worked on Wednesday and Thursday. It was simple. On Monday everyone was hung over, on Friday they were already gone and on Tuesday they were warming up for the week. That left Wednesday and Thursday to actually get things done. He watched the pedestrian traffic pass on the sidewalk and found himself singing out loud; "Walking in LA. Nobody walks in LA." He laughed staring at the women. He had always heard California women were the most beautiful. He wondered if a Texas ten was really an LA eight. How could you tell? So many women and not many cracking a five he thought. He turned up the radio to distract himself.

Adler's law office was in a small office park. The front door was on a short sidewalk, just off the main sidewalk with parking in the back. Roger started making notes; "Modest signage, all matching, including painted names on the glass next to the main door." His scribbles we clear but only to him. No one came or went for the hour and a quarter he sat there watching.

At noon a Hispanic woman exited Adler's office and locked the door. He would have noticed her even if he was not there to watch that office. She was tall, five foot seven or something less than that because she was wearing heels. Six inches he guessed, but that was his "y" chromosome estimating. They were actually two and she was five foot four. Long raven black hair was tucked into a bun. She was wearing a two-piece pants suit in a matching navy blue that was too tight for her. She had already planned to put it in the donation pile when she got home, but Roger would have voted against that. "So." Roger said out loud to no one in particular. "We have a key huhn? My money says Secretary."

Darlene Diaz was dressed in a black pant suit, not the navy blue Roger thought but it had faded from age. She wore a white puffy blouse that hid her ample bosom. The blouse was faded from too many trips through the washer to a slight grey that bothered her even though she was the only one that really noticed. She had "hips" as she sometimes said, a term she used to imply that there was nothing she could do about it. In a fat America, she looked thin.

"I'm no different than some movie stars or singers." She once told an ex, "A lot of them are a bit chunky too."

It was a speech she gave herself many times but it did nothing to stop her from thinking she was fat. It was a private thought she did not share with anyone fearing they may reject her. Her hair was in a large wide pony tail, not the bun Roger thought.

She pulled the hair tie as she walked so she could comb it out and twist it back after lunch. A few quick strokes with the brush in her desk drawer at the bathroom mirror while she checked her makeup, a lunch routine that was comforting. A simple gold bracelet, a gift from the former and necklace she bought for herself last Christmas completed her "work look."

She walked at text pace, a term she did not know

but everyone lived. She was not in a hurry to walk down the street to Tony's Tacos. She never wore a watch and never felt like she was in a hurry. As usual, her phone was glued to her left hand.

"South bound," Roger thought as she turned into the familiar taco house on the corner. Roger loved being a cop again even if he really wasn't. He jumped out of the car forgot to lock it and quickly got to the corner catching the walk light. He crossed and entered the taco house so he could stand behind her. His mind distracted from his normal observation about how little crap joints like this could get an A from the Health Department. He looked her in his usual fashion, wedding ring, none. Nice.

"Is this place fast?" He asked. "I'm in a bit of a hurry."

"Yeah." She said unaware he followed her. She has kind eyes he thought. "Is it good?" He pressed.

"Yeah," she said. "I come here all the time."

Roger had to focus, "kind eyes," would not be a good description in the small report he planned to write for Jack. Make up was important to girls. She was wearing "LA make up" which meant a lot but her dark Hispanic skin meant she did not need foundation. Two colors of mascara or eyeliner whatever they called it. Wow, he thought her eyes were wild, this girl paid attention to detail.

"What's good?" Roger asked, and then followed quickly with "Sorry if I'm bothering you, I'm not from around here".

"Pretty much everything." She said as she looked back at him thinking about a recommendation.

"I'm from Texas," Roger said having moved forward and to her left the perfect 14" that allowed him to look across at her, but not appear to close.

"I am here for my job, and so far, all I have done is eat with my boss." He smiled attempting to look innocent.

"'its okay." she said, glancing at him between checking texts. Roger noticed that her keys were dangling from her phone hand.

If he was a threat she could poke him in the eyes with the keys, smart he though and given the size of the key chain it would work. The key chain was a single word "Dance" made from some type of well worn metal or plastic.

"Hey, last question I promise." He said, again with his "trust me" smile. "Do you happen to know a good dance club around here; I gotta get out of the hotel."

"What kind?" she asked.

"What?" Roger said not thinking she would ask for details. "Oh, it doesn't matter." He said catching himself before he said Salsa because it would make him look like a stalker.

"I am just sick of sitting in the damn hotel room. I gotta get out somewhere and bars are well, you know." Shooting his third "trust me" smile.

"There is a Western place in San Bernardino I think. It's an old bowling alley or something like that, and one in San Dimas, a few swing clubs but there not open every night. There is a little Salsa place called Pepitas. I actually teach lessons there sometimes."

"No kidding." Roger said interrupting her. 'Jack pot' he thought to himself as she turned to order. A clerk came to a second cash register for the lunch rush and gestured to Roger asking what he wanted.

"I'll have two chicken tacos to go." He paid and

glanced around while he waited. It was clean and familiar. He had been in a thousand places like it before. He hoped the two tacos would be slow so he could think of something interesting to say.

"This place is sure clean." He said after waiting for Darlene to look his way. "Reminds me of my regular place back home."

"Are you from San Antonio?" She asked fully turning to look at him. "I know some people in San Antonio."

"Nope, big D, little A, double L, AS" he said immediately regretting it."

"Oh," she said.

You sound like an idiot he thought to himself. He grabbed the taco's glad they were fast.

"Hey thanks, maybe I will see you at Pepitas." He said, "I gotta find someplace." He didn't wait for her to respond. "Sure" she said as he took baby steps toward the door. Roger planned to camp out at Pepitas until he found her. Standard page two in the book of cop.

Roger walked quickly to the Suburban. Nice work he thought, "Creep factor zero." He jumped in the truck took out his note pad jotted down the essentials.

He underlined "Killer Zapata's" chuckling because he knew Jack would never read it. The only note that mattered was Pepitas. He pulled his phone and Duck Duck Go gave him the address. It was in a city called West Covina, an outbuilding in a large mall near the ten freeway. Perfect he thought sliding the phone to map mode to figure out how to get back to the Beverly Hills.

Chapter Six

Adler drove his Mercedes Diesel through the porte-cochere and parked on the back slab in front of the garage. He waved at the day nurse and let himself into the large but dated home through the kitchen door. The home was built in the true Spanish style of the late 1950's with small arches and clay roofs before machine stucco. It was a real ranchero, grand in its day with five bedrooms and nearly 4,000 square foot on a half acre in a suburb of Los Angeles called Arcadia.

Arcadia was famous for horse racing at Santa Anita. In the 1930's when land was cheap those with means built little rancheros near the race track to stable horses. In the modern LA megalopolis the land alone was worth millions. Arcadia was a favorite spot for developers because Arcadia was one of the few cities in Los Angeles County where yesterday's horse people were today's developers.

Two horse lots could be turned into a cul-de-sac of nine two story homes with postage stamp lawns. Los Angeles's growing population produced a never ending demand for high end homes and high end prices that had no ceiling. Adler knew the formula cheap labor based on liberal border policies and "sanctuary city" status supported legal exploitation of the newly arrived Mexicans working for the older arrived Mexicans. Paying millions for empty land was money in the bank.

Adler spent several years counseling and courting Dorothy and Donald Williams so that one day he could take their land and cash in on all those years of effort. Dottie had outlived Donald but her enlarged heart was wearing out so Adler decided it was pay day.

Dottie's Congestive heart failure produced a

persistent cardiac arrhythmia. She wanted to have bypass surgery to clear her mostly clogged coronary arteries but Adler advised her not to do it. He knew it would extend Dottie's life, but that wouldn't work for him.

Adler told her the doctors said she was too frail for the procedure and would die on the operating table. He showed her the consent form she would have to sign that said she was taking the risk of death, knowing it would scare her. Besides, medication would work just as well.

Her prescriptions were genuine and common. Lasix, Digoxen and Benazepril, the once "standard cocktail" for the elderly. Adler had seen Benazepril before but could not remember what it was for. Lasix was a vasodilator allowing the heart to pump easier and Digoxen worked to slow the rhythm of the muscle that defined life. The drugs were perfect for a heart that was trying to force blood through clogged coronary arteries. The pills, all personally delivered by Adler were complete with bag and receipt from the local Walgreens but Adler had replaced the prescribed medication with a cocktail he developed himself.

"Trust," Adler had once told the Williams, "is a lawyer's only tangible product, the rest is argument and knowledge." It was nonsense but it sounded good and the Williams trusted their friend and attorney.

It did not take Adler long to develop his special brand of prescriptions it was the only real "MO" he had stuck with. After attempting to cultivate and grow his own strain of infectious bacteria from fecal matter he mixed with mayonnaise and incubated he was left unhappy with the lethality, or lack of lethality he created.

Making people sick was not going to work they seemed to always have the time to get medical attention and heal. He needed a faster way to end the lives of his "special" clients. While watching a commercial that pushed some new drug that would make "big pharma" millions he realized he had a unique advantage, boxes of left over pills from a broad collection of deceased clients with different medical problems. Patients that had medication for a fast heart had their pills swapped with patients that had slow hearts.

Adler purchased a physical copy of the Physician's Desk Reference which was a giant book that listed all the drugs made with details about what they did and better for him, what dangers they posed if mixed with other drugs.

Adler opted out of the on line version after debating how he could explain it should he face suspicion. "Contraindicated" became Adler's favorite word. It meant simply that the drug had a proven negative effect and told you exactly how to avoid it or for him, make it happen. He quickly concluded that chronic medical problems could not be used to cause death or at least not in the time he wanted.

Adler's usual "case load" of twenty patients and leftovers from the deceased gave him ample drug options. Wherever possible Adler asked for the prescriptions to be filled with caplets. He once remarked to a pharmacist. "So many of these pills are too large for my elderly clients to swallow." An obvious point no one would argue.

Medication that could not be obtained in caplets worried him so he sanded off the identifying marks numbers and symbols that seemed present on all hard tablets. It always surprised him that no one made an effort to look up the drugs on the internet. It would have been very easy to get caught.

Home nurses, or "caregivers" always got sanded tablets even though they were most often people who didn't have the "mental temerity" to catch him. Adler relied on trust and his image to manipulate people. His patients never thought that they should check on him.

In the six years Adler had been working for his cause only one person ever gave him any reason to pause. A recently arrived Pilipino women near her fifties asked why the pills seemed "Thinner and looked different." Adler said he would check with the pharmacy but she never got an answer.

Before she could start her next shift Adler dismissed the company and in a verbal tirade he was quite proud of, he lambasted the owner for hiring someone who stole several valuable items from the client's home. Accusations, even if they were lies were a good buffer preventing more questions. Psychopaths often use the same tactic, but Adler denied that too. He boasted that he could prosecute then slowly said he didn't have enough evidence to link a specific nurse to the theft.

He rejected the offer for a discount and then as planned, softened his voice and warned the owner to "Check her people more carefully." He knew she would accept his reassuring tone as a signal that it was over. The image of an angry lawyer that could sue you would keep her quiet. He felt safe inside the stereotype to do what he wanted.

Within a week Mrs. Thomas had passed. Even if his anger did not work and the nurse pressed her point with the police Mrs. Thomas was cremated as specifically stated in her Will.

A Will Adler had written knowing there was little evidence in ashes.

"How is she doing?" Adler said a thick concerned tone to his voice bolstering his image for the day nurse knowing today was her last day.

"Fine, she didn't eat much, that's not good." Said a large boned heavily accented Hispanic woman in standard blue scrubs sitting at the kitchen table.

"Well, I can take over, why you don't take off a little early." Adler said. "I can make her some soup." He saw the nurse out and walked into Mrs. William bedroom. She was lying on the bed asleep as usual.

"Dottie you have not eaten. I am going to start an IV to get some fluid in you, can't be dehydrated you know what the doctor said about that." Adler said as he started the IV in a nearly unconscious Mrs. Williams.

She was lying on her back wearing her favorite night gown. It was thread bare white cotton that turned gray over time with a few embroidered flowers at the seam near her shoulders. She called it a Muumuu and he was smart enough not to argue with her.

Adler slowly injected two milligrams of epinephrine that he had taken from his stock pile, a left over vile from a careless ambulance driver after a 911 call. Adler felt for a pulse but had a difficult feeling it.

Somewhere between 130 and 150 he surmised. She did not respond which surprised him but he concluded she was closer to death than he thought. He moved forward with his plans injecting four more milligrams. He was trying to induce Super Ventricular Tachycardia and sustain it for several minutes. An "SVT" is a heat rate of 160 or greater. In a person with an irritable damaged heart with blocked coronary arteries like Mrs. Williams, it was serious. Her heart moved less than half the blood it did when she was twenty nine. The faster the heart pumps the more oxygen it needs but blocked coronary arteries limited the amount of fresh blood the heart could get. Muscle cells starved of oxygen start to infarct if you went to medical school or simply a heart attack if you didn't. It is an emergency everyone could recognize.

Millions of muscle cells make up the human heart. A beautiful redundancy that easily makes one believe in a divine creator but there are limits. If a myocardial infarction lasts long enough the damage becomes an irregular heart rhythm. Adler thought rhythm was an odd word for a heat rate. Rhythm is often used to talk about music. America might run on rock and roll but an irregular heart is not a tune anyone wants to hear.

In quiet bedrooms from lighthouses on the coast of Maine through the prairies and past the Golden Gate symphonies of labored hearts echoed sad slow ballads far from rock and roll.

Adler watched and waited. He wanted to hear her saliva pool and gurgle. The "death rattle" some say but to Adler it was the sound of money. "Ooh." she said, slowly moving a frail skinny arm to her chest as her heart raced past 160 toward its final beat.

Chapter Seven

Pepitos Cantina and Dancing was easy to find and as common and clichéd as most Mexican restaurants in Texas Roger thought as he walked in doing his standard toggle head survey of the joint. Rustic wooden chairs with bright multicolored inserts that looked like garage sale rejects were leaning awkwardly next to worn tables. Plastic or perhaps some type of brightly colored resin parrots posed to look like they were perched in multiple clumps made the place look cheap. Rod iron chandeliers, a few with wire nuts partly wrapped with electrical tape covered each table next to walls with larger less appealing chandeliers, including one in the middle of the restaurant. Obligatory tin signs proclaiming that Dos Equis and Tecate were "Muy bueno" completed the nothing new interior.

The building was in the middle of some place called Toluca Lake. Roger ignored the annoyance that the city had lake in the name but there was no lake nearby. Back home if a place had lake in the title there was a real lake somewhere. Toluca Lake had mostly high-rise glass boxes. Modern Los Angeles Roger thought, ditch the lake build another cement box.

Pepitos seemed to have an enclosed patio or maybe it was an old garage they converted to the dance floor because you had to step down to get on it.

The parquet wooden floor was glued to concrete. Roger was sure it would float away if there was a flood, but he didn't think it rained much in Los Angeles.

Darlene and her friend Jennifer were regulars. They had landed their usual table before Roger arrived. The table was pushed against the wall and was close to the railing of the dance floor next. Jennifer had taken the seat he wanted facing the front door. Some cop thoughts never left you. Darlene sat across from her facing the dance floor. The only open seat was bad. His back would be to the front door. "Suck it up" he thought as he put on a smile grabbing the seat next to Darlene. His neck was going to get sore from swiveling.

"Hi." Roger said happy to see a smile on Darlene's face. He sat quickly so they couldn't say no. Darlene introduced Jennifer.

"How are the Margaritas in this place?" Roger asked in a loud raspy voice as if he had just rolled in from a walk across the desert. He had spent the day tracking down documents both at the courthouse and at the County Recorder's office. He was tired and hot and felt like having a good night out.

"Good." Jennifer said still sizing up the new guy. "We meet at lunch the other day." Roger offered to Jennifer.

Roger easily recalled the covert operations training he had before his temper got him sent to work the jails. Talked about the food, the weather, anything simple to look like a "good guy." He asked what the girls were drinking and took a chance ordering for everyone when the waitress with no name tag arrived. He looked at Darlene who nodded approval, and Jennifer who repeated her order not allowing Roger that type of control. No need to guess who's in control Roger thought to himself, she is…good to know.

"Is there a dance lesson? Roger asked.

"No." Darlene said, "But I can teach you some basics."

"I will take you up on that but you might regret

it, it could take some time." Roger said, in a sheepish tone. He waited for her to nod and then cut her off before she could speak. "Something like a year, I'm terrible."

Darlene laughed. "It's not that hard." She said with a smile.

"For you." Roger said emphasizing the "ou" sound suspecting she wouldn't take the compliment. "How often do you come here?" Roger asked the first of a million attentive questions about dancing, the club and superficially her life. Roger was working but he couldn't help himself from having a genuine interest in the dark haired Californian Bonita.

As the night passed Roger forgot the reason he was there. He went dancing a little before his first marriage but he didn't think doing the "muscle bound shuffle" was really dancing. The fake interest he offered about dancing evaporated as he learned the basic steps from Darlene. He wanted to get it right. Back in Texas, dancing meant one thing trying to hook up. Hooking up for the sake of hooking up, not for 'connecting.' Roger was not sure connecting ever happened at a loud dance club but that was because he had never done it and did not know it was happening to him at a cliché club called Pepitas in no lake city.

The loud music was perfect it gave him the excuse he wanted to get close to Darlene. "What?" he would say, then lean into her neck face at an angle to hear. He was inside her safe space but not a threat.

He danced almost every dance with Darlene practicing the basics she showed him trying not to make a fool of himself. Twice she asked him to dance with Jennifer. It could have been courtesy, it could have been a 'wingman fly by.' He knew the game. He was sure to smile and tell Jennifer she was a good dancer. Jennifer was heavier than Darlene and not attractive so he was careful not to pay too much attention to her.

"Chick code," he once told a friend is easy to understand. The less attractive girls signal the good looking ones to back off if they felt they had a chance with a new guy. The good looking ones always did it because they get so much more action they don't need to trap every guy. Roger needed to signal "not interested" to Jennifer while not looking like an ass. Jennifer was skilled at being a wingman, or "wing woman." She was sizing Roger up and he knew it. The few times they danced she asked the expected questions.

Roger couldn't tell you what they were, but his answers were all the same. "I am a model of trust and tolerance. I am flexible, easy going, generous and fair. I love to support and protect, but I would never think of controlling anyone, much less a strong woman." It was chapter two in his playbook, First date 101, if he ever actually wrote a play book. It was not about the truth. It was never about the truth.

"It's nice to be out." Roger said. "I am still getting over the death of my Dad."

"Oh, I'm sorry." Darlene said. Heartfelt concern on her face. "Was it recent?"

"Almost a year." Roger said. "But it is still hard."

"How did he die?" She asked.

"Scuba diving accident." Roger said.

"Oh, that is so dangerous." Darlene offered, not knowing much about it other than what she saw on TV.

"Yeah, well it was kind of a freak accident." Roger said. "He was diving an ancient wreck in the

Bahamas. In fact it was just inside the Bermuda Triangle. He was a photographer and he was focused on filming. There was a boat accident up on the surface and a boat was sinking right where the old wreck was. He didn't look up to see it and a piece of the sinking ship hit him on the head and knocked him out. He never saw it coming."

"Oh my God." Darlene said. "That's terrible."

"Yeah, but at least he died doing what he loved, and there was no way to see it coming. I mean who would have thought there would be two boat wrecks one right on top another older one."

"That's crazy. How old was he?" Darlene asked still concerned.

It was crazy Roger thought and if you were a little smarter you would know I made it up. The Bermuda Triangle - how much more obvious did I have to be? The sincere concern on Darlene's face stopped Roger from telling her it was a joke, so he just said "58." And then felt bad that he lied.

"How about your Mom?" Darlene asked.

"She died a couple years ago, Cancer. She was the best Mom ever. How about you?" Roger asked knowing her answer would tell him if his effort to cozy up to her was working.

"Yes. I live with her. I don't know what I would do without her." Darlene said without hesitation.

"I'm in." Roger thought. He continued to ask her simple questions as the hours disappeared faster than the margaritas.

When Jennifer began to play with her keys Roger knew it was a signal that she was getting ready to leave. He excused himself with the comment that he hoped there wasn't a line at the bathroom. He made quick work of the rest room to make sure they wouldn't leave without telling him. The "Goodbye" was the most important part.

He returned to the table where Jennifer was standing, keys in her hand. It was nice meeting you she said before he could sit.

"You're not leaving are you?" Roger said, knowing the answer.

'I have to go check on my Nephews, their Mom works nights and I have to make sure they are good.

"Oh, okay" Roger said, knowing he had to say something polite to get rid of her. "I get it, that's nice of you." She smiled and left. Roger sat down in the chair facing the door. "She's nice." He said, nodding his head toward Jennifer. Darlene smiled.

"Do you want to dance, or maybe go grab some coffee?" Roger said making sure his tone was level for both choices.

"Sure." Darlene said.

Roger's head tilted like a confused retriever. "Yes dance, or yes coffee? Or maybe we should dance at the coffee joint." Roger said happy to have Darlene alone.

Darlene laughed. "Coffee would be nice."

"Not that I need to sober up from the Margaritas, but coffee sounds great." Roger said slurring the word 'sober' to make her laugh. He stood and extended his arm for her to take it. She did but the place was small so they had to exit single file. That was enough for Roger to know the touch barrier had been passed. "I have a rental, but no clue where we could go."

"Are you hungry? I know some places. Darlene said.

"I could eat, but if you give me directions I will

get lost unless you want to just ride with me, I can run you back here."

"Sure." She said. Roger extended his arm again as they hit the sidewalk where Roger kept up his image of the caring yet soft protector. "Watch out for the tree." he said grabbing her arm and pulling her close even though they were several feet away from the Ficus tree the city planted to add some green in the concrete carpet.

Darlene directed Roger to a little place that didn't look much different than a Denny's. He didn't know if she went there a lot and he didn't care. They sat talking about nothing and laughing at stupid things. So far as anyone could tell they had known each other forever.

"I know who you remind me of, Max." Darlene said as if she had just remembered his name.

Roger hated being compared to old boyfriends he made it a point to never talk about exes. But she had a look on her face so he knew he had to let her lead.

"Who's Max? " He asked.

"A Chuweenie I rescued from the pound such sad eyes you both have." Darlene said with a laugh.

"Oh, Roger said smiling again. "Maybe I'll make you my bitch." He instantly regretted it and reminded himself that he was working and shouldn't be stupid.

"No, no she said laughing. I pull the leash I don't wear them."

"Oooh." Roger said, shaking his head and making a whimpering sound like a puppy. Then he leaned in and kissed her. No slap he thought. I guess I got away with stupid.

"Whoa" He said looking at his phone, surprised that it was a little after two. "It's getting late." he said.

"What, do you need some beauty sleep?" Darlene

poked "Where are you staying anyway." She asked, eyelids starting to sag.

"The Beverly Hills Hotel."

"Bullshit." Darlene said with an energetic exclamation in her voice.

"No, it's true my boss is a rich guy. He and his girlfriend are having a mini vacation here while she is working. She is a lawyer.

"I always wanted to see that place." Darlene said.

"Anytime." Roger responded "Its first class for sure. They even have one of those toilets that shoot water up your butt."

"A bidet?" Darlene asked even more excited than before. "I always wanted to try one of those."

"Oh, now I get it. You are using me for my toilet, while I get what…puppy pads." Roger said laughing.

"Of course." Darlene said drawing it out for effect.

Roger opened his phone to Google Maps, selected previous places, and in a few seconds he was told to turn right. "Can you hold it for nineteen minutes?" He said hitting the gas to pretend it was an emergency.

Roger pushed the voice command on the car while they drove. "Call the Beverly Hills Hotel. As the phone connected, he turned to Darlene

"I'm going to get a night cap sent to the room. Margaritas, Kahlua and Cream, Brandy, what do you want?" Roger asked.

"I don't know. Kahlua sounds good." Darlene said.

Roger was 'large and in charge,' something he and Jack had talked about before. Women liked a man who was large and in charge until they didn't, and knowing when they "didn't" was a well kept secret.

It did not take as long as Google predicted to get to the hotel, or at least it seemed that way. They spent the time talking about LA and Roger's impression of the place as they drove. Kahlua, fresh cream, Riesling and a fifth of Gentleman Jack was in his room just as he asked.

That wine looks good she said looking around the room. Roger opened the wine and poured her a glass, handing it too her as she stood at the window looking at the view of the city lights. Roger moved behind her looking out the window and lightly kissed the top of her head. "Crazy aint it?" He asked turning to pour the whiskey which made the familiar sound of ice cracking as he poured.

"Wow" Darlene said looking at the city. She turned and looked into his eyes. He couldn't read her, but the turn was enough. He kissed her again, just hard enough so she could run. He backed off, but she moved forward kissing him harder. He stopped long enough to sip his drink and put it on the table. He took the wine glass from her hand, and turned putting it on the table within her reach. As he moved in for the next kiss he whispered "No means no."

"I know." Darlene said.

"You're going to love the Egyptian cotton." He said. He had no idea what that meant and he had no idea what the sheets were made of. He heard about Egyptian cotton on a commercial and thought it sounded classy. Darlene didn't say anything, she was too busy kissing....

Roger rolled over in bed trying to delay the inevitable morning run to the bathroom until his head shrank a little. He knew it wouldn't work so he got up and made his way to the toilet.

He grabbed the old wall phone before he finished and ordered coffee, "No, no just the coffee." He said glancing at the robe. It felt weird but he tried it on anyway.

He was sitting naked under the robe in a desk chair glancing at his phone when she said "Good morning," scooting to the bathroom.

"There's a robe in there if you want it." He said as the shower pounded a familiar morning song into the tub bouncing off the balloon he was carrying on top his shoulders.

He grabbed a bottle of water and guzzled a little looking around for aspirin wondering why he felt hung over when he hadn't really drank that much the night before. Darlene came out of the Bathroom dressed. Roger was blowing on a cup of hot coffee when she came out.

"I found the coffee maker." he said gesturing.

"Oh." Darlene said looking. "Maybe a quick one. My son Gabriel has a soccer game, and I need to get going." She grabbed her phone to call an Uber.

"No problem." Roger said jumping up and walking toward the bathroom. "Give me a minute to grab some deodorant."

"Oh, that's okay, I can get an Uber." Darlene said. Glancing up from her phone.

He took a few steps toward her and gave her a quick kiss. "Are you dumping me?"

"No, God no." Darlene said.

"Good. I got nothing to do. I can run you to your car; just let me brush my teeth." He said wanting to smack her on the butt but decided against it as he walked to the bathroom for a quick tune up.

"I'm at your service." Roger said through garbled tooth paste as he walked around the room looking for fresh clothes.

"Let's go." He said, grabbing his keys trying to ignore the kettle drum on his shoulders that he wanted to fill with coffee. Within a few minutes he was following the directions the phone offered to take him to Darlene's car.

"It makes more sense that I take you to the game. That way we have time for a quick cup of coffee." He said, not sure he would argue if she disagreed.

"Sounds good." she said hand shading her eyes with one hand like a visor. Roger wasted no time pulling into the closest place, knowing he would spend the whole day to spend with her. Work was the last thing on his mind.

Coffees in hand, Darlene lead the way. "There he is number 14, Gabriel."

"He's a good looking kid." Roger commented just glancing at the boy.

They sat on the grass and watched without talking much, Darlene made the usual "ohs and ahs, as the game progressed." Roger was enjoying the cool morning weather more and more as his head shrunk back to normal size.

Darlene didn't tell Roger how Gabriel got to the game. Roger guessed it was the Dad. As the game ended and Darlene walked toward the team group she gestured to Roger to follow.

"Gabriel" Darlene she getting his attention. He ran over and said "Hi Mom."

Darlene grabbed Roger's hand and said "This is Roger." to Gabriel.

"Hi" he said less than interested.

"Nice game." Roger said as another boy yelled "Gabriel."

"Nice meeting you Gabriel." Roger said gesturing toward the boy because he knew Gabriel wanted to play with his friends.

"Unhuhn." Gabriel said followed quickly by "Stop it." to the friend who had kicked the ball at Gabriel making him turn to kick it back.

"Gabriel" Darlene started but Roger grabbed her arm. "Give him a second." Roger said. Darlene looked at Gabriel. "Kids" Roger added in an understanding tone with a nod of his head. Darlene understood but was frustrated. She turned to Gabriel who was already too far way to hear her. "See you tonight." She said her voice trailing as she realized he was too distracted to pay attention to his Mom.

They started walking toward Rogers's car without much thought he reached for her hand.

"I have to go to dinner with my boss and his girlfriend, but there is plenty of time to run you to your car.

"Your boss makes you eat dinner with him on a Saturday?" She asked.

"Well, I don't really have to but we always have fun and it beats grabbing a cold sandwich."

"Wow. He sounds way cooler than my boss." She said.

"A bad one huhn? I've had plenty of those." Roger said knowing she would talk more about her boss.

"He is a jerk and grumpy most of the time and silent when he is not grumpy. Silent guy is better, and always better than yelling or lecturing guy." She said.

"Been there." Roger said. "I punched one of my

bosses."

"Wow, I don't have that kinda guts." Darlene said.

"It was a mistake." Roger said. "I got demoted." She looked at him. "Cop" he said, knowing she would understand.

"You look like a cop." She said.

"If you want you can go with but I don't want to mess up any plans you might have."

"I should study for my finance class. You reminded me talking about my boss. That's my ticket out of there."

"Finance?" Roger asked, "You look like an accountant." He said laughing.

"No." Darlene said pointing to her face. "No glasses. Money is too important to think you know what you're doing so I took a class." She said. "I liked it and now I am four classes away from a degree in finance."

"Wow, that's cool." Roger said. Surprised at her devotion and then asked what kind of job she could get away from the bad boss."

"I don't know it's just community college. But they taught me about the time value of money. Do you know who much interest costs you?"

"No, I just make the payments." Roger said.

"It's a lot." Darlene said. Confidently.

"You could be a stock broker." Roger offered.

"Oh no. My Boss has tried that. He lost tons." Darlene said.

"Really." Roger said casually. "Doesn't he make a lot of money?"

"Yes, but he loses more. I saw his account once he lost more than a million dollars. I couldn't believe it. Do you know what I could do with a million dollars? It would set me up for life." Darlene said.

"Well if he was good at it you would lose your job." Roger offered trying to look on the bright side.

"Oh, I wish. I have almost quit that place like four times." Darlene said voice s till on edge.

"Wow?" Roger said then wondered how he was going to tell her they had a case with her boss.

"He just treats people bad. If he didn't pay so much I would already be gone." Darlene said.

"That bad huhn?" Roger asked.

"Yeah, he puts the Ass in Asshole that's for sure." Darlene added.

"Sounds like you have a plan to get out. That's the good news." Roger said smiling at her. Happy he had a report for Jack.

"Darlene smiled too." It felt good to have a nice man care about her.

Chapter Eight

Los Angeles was a never ending strip mall that appeared in every direction further than a drone could fly on a full charge. Roger refused to learn the names of neighborhoods referring to all of them as "Stack-'em and Stuff-'em Stuccos," which was hard to forget. Most restaurants regardless what type of food they served specialized in stuffing as many people as possible into tables that were too small and too close. If you wanted to eat a nice dinner in Los Angeles away from people you didn't know, you better get famous.

Landmarks like the Playboy mansion, the Polo Club, Chasens, and endless shops and businesses on Wilshire Boulevard were either gone or deteriorating their way toward history. Restaurants made famous by movies and T.V. shows did not always make it to reruns. Jack wanted to go to Nobu but it was in Malibu and the time it took to get there meant it would take all day. Distance didn't matter in LA, time was the only measurement. Local favorites like Pink's Hot Dogs survived but it was not the kind of dinner Jack thought he and Jennie would have when he was pushing her to take the probate case so they could have an "LA vaca."

Sitting at the Palms Jack ordered Ice Tea for four. He was following a "No drinks before 4pm" rule and wanted to give Roger some instructions before he forgot. Drinking got in the way of thinking and that was a universal truth everyone found out the next day, often when it was too late.

Jack and Jennie were waiting on the tea when Roger and Darlene walked in fresh from an afternoon together that included a quick trip to Darlene's house to get her best Beverly Hills outfit.

"Hey guys, this is Darlene, the girl I have been

telling you about." Roger said, casually sliding into the booth next to Jack.

"Hi, I'm Jack." Jack said with a short wave because he was too far to shake hands.

"Hi." Darlene said, instinctively turning to Jennie at her left.

"I'm Jennie."

"Roger told me you are a lawyer." Darlene said.

"Yes, I am here for a probate case from Texas." Jennie answered.

"Texas? Is it Rachel Haddon?" Darlene asked surprised.

"Yes, how did you know?" Jennie asked.

"That's my boss's case. This is the first time we had anyone from out of state and I remembered Texas." Darlene said.

"Oh, well then we won't talk about the case. But your boss seems like a nice guy." Jennie said eager to prove Jack wrong.

"He is an asshole." Darlene said shaking her head no.

"Whoa." Jennie said surprised.

"So much for first impressions." Jack said looking at Jennie to make a point. She glanced at him but looked back to Darlene ignoring the inference.

"Roger says you have a son." Jennie asked.

"Yes, Gabriel." He is nine.

"Wow." Jennie said, subtly complimenting Darlene who looked younger than she was. "Is that a good age? What is he like?"

"He is a good boy but sometimes, oh my God I just want to smack him. What he needs is a father to show him how to be a man."

"Hard to find a man in this soft ass town." Roger

offered flexing. Darlene waved a hand at him bending only at the wrist as if to swat him away then turned back to Jennie.

"He was angry because I won't get him the unlimited cellular plan." Darlene said.

"Ah." Jennie said understanding.

"Take the phone away." Roger said. "He doesn't need it."

"Oh my gosh, typical man, solves the problem just like that." Darlene said twisting her fingers in a snapping movement that made no sound. "You don't think about safety. What if something happened to him? He has to have a way to contact me" Darlene said looking at Jennie.

"Does he spend much time with his father?" Jennie asked. Careful how she phrased the question.

"No, I was young and stupid but I tell everyone; you know, I got a beautiful boy and I learned my lesson. Next time I will get a good man." Darlene said then glanced at Jennie adding "You probably heard that before."

"You might, I'm still thinkin' bout it." Roger said twanging his voice like a TV Texan to make it obvious he was complimenting himself.

"Stop." Darlene said exaggerating her Spanish accent. "You are such a trouble. Do you see what I have to put up with? Is he always like this?"

"Usually worse." Jennie said, a first shot that Roger thought was overdue.

"He is a good kid. I showed him how to do pushups, and the right way too, not from your knees." Darlene said. "I don't do pushups from my knees." She added looking at Roger obviously referring to a conversation they had before.

"Darlene, it's not you. Roger is motivated by a deep desire to antagonize all women." Jennie said, taking her second shot at Roger that he knew would not be her last.

"That's not true. I am motivated by several things, aren't I?" Roger said looking at Darlene, an awkward reference Jennie ignored.

"What motivates you Roger?" Jennie asked. Roger knew it was a setup question, and that Jennie was on Darlene's side. He thought of telling her that she was making an "Obvious attempt to be Darlene's wingman but that "wing night" was Thursdays, so she was out of luck." but decided to play along instead.

"Women and whiskey." He offered with a smile.

"Here we go." Jack said out loud.

"Oh that's deep." Jennie said mocking Roger. So you're looking for what, a stripper that can hold her whiskey."

"You know any?" Roger said, flashing a guilty grin. Then added. Rum's fine too, plus you get rank.

"That's a self-centered view of the world don't ya think." Jennie fired back looking at Darlene.

"Rank, what rank?" Jack asked, not knowing that Roger had suckered him.

Roger leaned back in the booth. Jack fell for his set up line and he was ready.

"I can't believe you don't know…Everybody knows when you drink rum you get to be a Captain." They didn't. Jack groaned.

"Captain Morgan Rum? Really a Dad joke."
"It for sure outranks any sergeant making whiskey."

Jack shook his head, Darlene giggled, and then Jennie laughed at the face Roger made to Darlene.

"You probably didn't know it, but Captain Crunch? He is not even in the military it's all marketing." Roger said.

"Darlene, Roger has a tough exterior but it looks like you found his soft center." Jack said "A soft soggy cereal center or maybe like a Cadbury Egg, Perhaps I should start calling you Cad."

Roger smiled he was happy to be the center of attention. It made him look good in front of Darlene.

"The same company owns Captain Crunch and Captain Morgan. They get you hooked as a kid then it's on to the hard stuff." Roger said wondering if Darlene would believe it, but she did not respond.

"We need a dad joke limit, don't you think Jack." Jennie said.

"Hey, if Jack picks we will be deep into who knows what before drinks are served." Roger replied.

"What?" Darlene asked. Roger glanced at Jack then looked at Darlene.

"Jack makes up bizarre puzzles like if there was a fire at the crematorium and they found five bodies how would you know who belong and who was dumped." Roger said glancing at Jack.

"If you figure it out let me know." Jack said.

"Don't they have records?" Darlene asked.

"Sure, but destroyed in the fire." Jack said tilting his head a little looking at Darlene.

"The answer is six." Roger said obfuscating the question. But before anyone could respond Roger changed the subject.

"I called my friend at the VA to see if Adler was in the Army like you thought. Turns out he was. In fact, he was a MOS35E." Roger said.

"What does that mean?" Jennie asked.

"He was a spook." Roger said.

"What's a spook?" Jennie asked

"A spy." Jack offered.

"Sort of a super spy." Roger said.

"Super spy?" Darlene asked. "I didn't even know he was in the Army."

"Well you have spies that get information secret cameras beating the hell out of people in the bright lights all that Hollywood crap. Not that I would ever do that." Roger said with an "I'm lying grin" to Darlene.

"Then you have 'spy's spies." Roger offered making quote marks with his fingers. He paused to see if they understood but they didn't. "Counter intelligence." He paused again. Same blank faces.

"What's the difference between a spy and a spook?" Jennie asked.

"The counter intelligence guys are spooks. They show up like a ghost, tell you a story then vanish." Roger said but there was no response. "You know D-day, the Manhattan Project and all that. It should have been obvious after all the guy is a lawyer. It only makes sense that he was a professional liar in the Army." Roger added.

"Hey." Jennie responded. Jacks eyes rolled slightly up in his head.

"Present company accepted." Roger said mistaking accepted from excepted with a nod of his head to Jennie. "And I don't mean that because you are a woman. Everyone knows women are supposed to be told they are equals."

"What do you mean told?" Jennie asked skipping the excepted mistake.

"Well, women are not really equal. They don't

work in oil fields like men do."

"Some do" Jennie fired back.

"Do you think your American point of view is the only one Jen? Do you really think everyone in the world thinks women are equals? There are cultures where women still walk a step behind and to the right?"

"Backward cultures." Jennie said.

"Backward to who?" Roger said. "What about Arabs they got tons of money and women have to cover their face." Roger said, adding, "Money is power."

"They have money because they have oil." Darlene said. "That doesn't make them smart."

"Money and power does not put you on the moral high ground." Jennie added.

"Moral high ground?" Roger chortled. Then he signaled for the waitress. "Round of Corona's with lime please." He said then turned back to Jennie.

"Where exactly is the moral high ground? Is it here in Los Angeles, maybe I can go there and see it for myself?"

"You know what I am talking about." Jennie responded. Jack though he should jump in and hit the pressure relief valve but he was too late.

"Jen." Roger said, tone much softer. "That's what I am talking about. That's American thinking. The Russians don't run around saying "Better not hoard the free milk we share so we can be on the moral high ground The Korean's don't say we are making so much money on cars we can afford to pay our workers more, because it's the moral thing to do."

"They should." Jennie said.

"Says the America." Roger replied extending his

palm.

"We are world leaders in ethics, equality and human rights. It is our job to lead the world both economically and morally." Jennie replied.

"You can't lead hungry people to the ethical road unless there is food there. That's why American Agriculture should be unregulated." Roger said.

"Fine. But you gotta cut the misogynist crap. Farming is a great example of where women are equal." Jennie said passionately.

"You don't see it do you?" Roger said.

"See what?" Darlene asked."

"Counter intelligence. All the stuff I just did was counter intelligence... You learn what "they" want, what "triggers" people use it to get them worked up while you stab them in the back with the other hand. I created a diversion to get you to agree on the farming regulation." Roger said satisfied that he had given them an example of a spook, but they did not respond.

"The whole point was for me to get you going about equality then slip in the unregulated Ag stuff that you agree too without thinking because you were focused on women's rights. That's counter intelligence I controlled you." Roger said.

"Listen to what you're saying." Jennie snapped back. "The logical application of what you saying is that people don't think. People are controlled by what social media?"

"No they are controlled by their priorities; spooks use that to play them. It's a game for lying bastards." Roger said.

"That makes sense." Darlene said.

"Really?" Roger said as the waitress arrived with four bottles of Corona Beer, lime twist in each neck casually placing them on the table. Roger grabbed his, twisted the lime into the beer and took a long drink.

"Everyone is hungry for something." Jack said. "And I usually know what it is… another round of drinks." He raised his beer and took another drink and exclaimed "Cheers." Roger took another drink as they all laughed. Jack discarded his lime and took a drink of the beer. He was happy his move to change the topic worked.

"Priorities are set by social media. It seems everybody posts things that make them look cool. It drives me crazy." Darlene said.

"Exactly." Roger said.

"I know a guy," Jack said. "Car painter. Completely color blind. His wife tells him what color to paint cars and they get along great. And Jen, what if some woman in some Arab country goes to bed every night thanking God that she has a husband who takes care of her? Lots of people in those countries, one of them has to be delighted. What would make you crazy might be perfect for her." Jack offered.

"What sharing a room with all his other wives." No thanks, that's not right. That is a universal wrong." Jennie said grabbing her beer and squeezed the lime into the neck. She noticed Roger staring at her intently. "What" she said giving him a scowl.

Roger looked at Darlene. "Not to be a dick, and not that I am saying I told you so or doing a victory lap." He stopped and took a drink of his beer as Darlene took a small drink with him. "But, I know you don't care about the Agriculture bill, so I also decided I would order some beers. I didn't ask you guys, and I ignored the fact that we said we would go out for margaritas just to try and prove sneaky crap can happen when you are manipulating people."

Roger looked up and caught the waitress's eyes. Four margaritas, two strawberries and two limes all blended all with salt." Then he looked at the group. "If that's all right with you guys." There was a pause. Jennie looked at her beer bottle then at Jack.

"Well I get it but I am not sure it would work with something bigger, like human rights. And despite the fact that some women are happy being a step behind the man I think they key is that they have a choice at least it is to me." Jack said tipping his beer bottle toward Roger like a nod of his head to the successful manipulation, then draining it.

"God." Darlene said a little thoughtfully. "That's a universal truth."

"No." Roger said, "Not with suicide bombers blowing themselves up for some jihad."

"That's not religion, that's insanity." Jennie shot back.

"Amen." Darlene added.

"What makes people crazy?" Jack asked.

"Social Media." Roger said. "People do stupid stuff and get pissed off when they don't have the same likes as the next guy. It should be banned." then he looked at Jennie and added, "Except for women." They all laughed.

"Social media gets people worked up with hysteria rather than fact. But I don't think you can ban it." Jennie said.

"The pain of being alone, of not belonging makes people do crazy things. They hide behind make-up or a suit like some of those people at the bar or they join a protest they don't even understand just to fit in." Jack said.

Jennie fidgeted in her chair. She did not like the conversation. It made her think that Jack knew things about her past. Things she didn't want him to know. Even when they were alone and she felt close she hadn't told him everything. No one had ever read her like Jack could but trust built slowly. She braced for him to turn to her and ask a probing question."

"That makes sense." Darlene said. "I don't go on social media much everybody has an opinion and if you disagree they just attack you."

"Everyone wants to connect, to matter. Why do you think Twitter is popular or X, whatever it is?" Jack asked. "Being alone is worse than starving to death it starves your soul. Look at Covid. Look at the pain and increased hatred that spilled into the internet. People will do damn near anything to avoid being alone." Jack said. "It makes me glad to be here with y'all." He raised his fresh margarita and waited for them to join him. "Regardless what we're drinking, here is to people that don't suck."

"For sure." Roger said quick lift of his glass followed by a quicker drink. "But I gotta drink a lot of these to think like you. You make being human sound like a trap."

"Damn the torpedoes full truth ahead." Jack said smiling and twisting a cliché about bravery none of them really understood. Then he drained his glass.

"Sorry boy's I think people are mostly good." Jennie said. "Take Darlene's Boss. You two think he is a bad actor." She said making air quotes, "But I bet he is an okay guy, right Darlene." Jennie said.

"Oh no." Darlene said without hesitation. "He is weirdo and he is mean too."

"Weirdo? how so?" Roger asked.

"He doesn't like sports, he doesn't date and he loses a ton of money in the stock market like it is nothing." Darlene said.

"Maybe he has a ton of money." Jennie offered.

"No. One time my paycheck was late. That really pissed me off." Darlene added quickly.

"Is he a Gambler?" Roger asked.

"No" Darlene said.

"The Stock Market is gambling if you think about it." Jack said.

"I hear him placing orders with his broker. Arguing with him about how he knows the stock is a winner. One time I wrote down the stock and went to see what it was selling for because I was going to buy some. Oh my good lord he lost more than $200,000 in one day." Darlene said.

"Wow." Jennie said.

"He was a pain in the ass after that let me tell you." Darlene said.

"Sounds like an idiot. Does he talk about who will play him in the movie?" Roger said laughing.

"What?" Darlene asked with her forehead crinkled in question.

"You don't see it do you?" Roger said, laughing that she fell into his trap.

"I'm not sure I see it either Roger?" Jennie added.

Roger smiled and looked at Jack. He was going to have a moment in front of his new girl and he wanted Jack to be in on it with him.

"Think about it. If they are making a movie about your crimes it means you got caught. The good criminals don't get movies because they don't get caught." Roger added with certainty.

Darlene smiled and Roger laughed looking at her then leaned in and whispered something giving her a casual kissed.

"I would tell you two to get a room but I know you already got one." Jack said glad the subject had changed. The comfort of a superficial topic lifted his mood like the Santa Anna winds blew pollution out of Los Angeles. Jacks' flirtation with talking about truth and the human condition was over. He was content to be part of the few that dared to look at the pain of being human and happy he knew when to look away.

"That's why I don't use Google around him." Roger said.

"What?"Darlene said not sure what Roger was talking about.

"Google spies on you. One time I got directions to a liquor store, I bought some whiskey and paid with a credit card then went home. Two hours later I start seeing all these ads for that Seen on TV stuff." Roger said.

"What seen on TV stuff?" Jennie asked.

"You know those non stick fry pans, the magnetic screen doors, food dice and slicer things, that kinda stuff. Google waited until it thought I was drunk enough to buy that crap then flooded me with the ads." Roger said.

"Wait, you probably bought one of those snuggly things. What do they call them, the blankets with arms?" Darlene asked looking at Jennie.

"Snuggies?" Jennie offered.

"Yeah, and your to manly to admit it. Probably bought thought the cammo colored one would make you look tough." Darlene poked at Roger. Roger laughed.

"First off, I don't think they make them in cammo, but if they did that would be cool. Secondly I would never buy one because they're crap. Probably as thin as this cocktail napkin." Roger said. Defensively looking at Jack for support. .

"You're strange but not the snuggie type." Jack said. "I tell you else I find strange is your boss Mr. Adler." Jack added looking at Darlene.

"He's a jerk." Darlene said. Using polite terms because she just meet them.

"All lawyers are jerks." Roger said, "Sept you." He added nodding to Jennie.

"I don't mean jerk, so much as strange." Jack said.

"You got that right." Darlene said, with a slight accent she wasn't aware of. Jack shook his head in a confused way.

"It's like he's hiding things." Darlene offered just as the food arrived. "It makes sense he was a spy."

"I suspect as much about the Haddon case. I would love to look at his old files and see if I can figure it out." Jack said thinking out loud.

"We could do that. He has a storage unit he never goes to, He orders me to go there but he never goes." Darlene offered.

"What's in the storage?" Jack asked.

"Old files and some sort of lung machine."

"A lung machine?' Jack asked confused as to why Adler would have one.

"Yeah." Darlene said opening her phone to show Jack the picture she took to make sure she put everything in the right order. "Look at this thing, it is so creepy." She turned her phone so that Jack could see the picture.

"That's not a lung machine." Jack said, "It's an incubator, an old one."

"I don't know many details. I don't waste my time doing an inventory unless he pays me but you can go look if you want." Darlene said with an edge to her voice.

"That could be interesting." Jack said.

"But it has to be on a Weekend." Darlene added

"Tomorrow is Sunday. I can keep you busy until then." Roger said shooting what he thought was a bad boy grin.

"Oh my God. Men." Darlene said turning to look at Jennie and talking with her fork. Roger laughed and held up his hands surrendering to the fork.

"It's no problem, I got a key." Darlene said more eager to co-operate than Jack was to look.

"Are you sure." Jack asked. She was.

Chapter Nine

Darlene opened the door to Adler's storage and walked in like she had dozens of times before. Jack noticed the incubator Darlene described the minute his eyes adjusted to the darker room. Layers of dust covered most of the boxes but not enough to cover the Staples and Iron Mountain labels on the sides. All of the boxes had black marked numbers on the side and top.

Jack opened the door to the incubator very slowly with two fingers careful not to disturb the thin dust that blunted the shiny metallic top. Inside he found a fold top baggie. It was old and had lost the flexibility he expected. He moved it carefully rolling the glass viles inside so he could read the name as Darlene glanced over his shoulder.

"Such-lo-line" Darlene said with a questioning tone.

"Succinylcholine" Jack said so softly that no one heard him. What was that doing here?

"What's it for?" Darlene asked.

"It's a muscle relaxer." Jack Said, "Only it's not something you can use."

"I'll take it." Roger said. "Hell I could use it, Darlene is a ball buster."

"It's for surgeries." Jack said ignoring Roger's joke. "Kinda like Curare."

"What's Curare?" Darlene asked.

"Well, if you are going to have surgery they knock you out, but then they have to paralyze you so you don't move like you do when you're asleep. That's what Curare does.

"Bullshit." Darlene said stunned.

"Google it." Jack responded still staring at the

baggie. "The real question is what the hell is it doing here?

"Who cares? The guy is probably some kinda dirt ball tweeter." Roger said.

Inside the incubator was another baggie. Jack debated picking it up because he knew the dust pattern would change and that Adler was the type of person who would notice. Roger grabbed the baggie he wasn't much for being subtle.

"What's this shit." Roger asked pawing a baggie up toward his face.

"Roger." Jack said. "Careful. I don't want Adler to know we were here."

"So." Roger said, "We will dust it all off and make it even. Helps with finger prints too." Roger unfolded the baggie, at his face level spilling the contents onto an empty spot of shelving making a sustained clatter like a pull behind child's toy that pops balls into a dome echoing through an empty hotel lobby.

"Dude." Jack said watching pills scatter.

"Let me get 'em." Roger said, bending to retrieve the pills.

Jack began sorting the pills; he had six groups until Roger retrieved a unique one from the floor making seven different types.

"He takes care of a lot of old people; these could be left over pills from them." Darlene said.

"What are they?" Roger asked.

"I don't know." Jack said.

"Google it." Roger replied laughing.

"Hey Google, what type of pills would a rich tweeker fuck want to keep from a bunch of old people." Roger was joking, but his phone beeped. They all laughed before Roger's phone said "Sorry I didn't get that."

Jack was looking at the pills. Rounds and ovals, nothing unusual. Three of the groups had numbers or letters sort of cast into them when they were made. Depressions below the surface of the pill. 357, AON, and 52. One had small specks of red. Then he noticed that one had a grove cut across the short part of the oval.

"Curare." Roger said, "That's the crap that was on those darts in Raiders of the Lost Ark. All them jungle dudes spitting darts at you that would kill your ass. That's where I heard of it. Adler was probably injecting himself with small amounts of that shit to get high. Is that what this is all about, just some freaky drug habit? Stealing from his clients to get high? Makes sense same story as a million other lost tweekers just with a tie."

"I don't know." Jack said. "Darlene said he lost lots of money in the stock market; maybe he was going to sell these. How much are they worth?" Roger asked.

"Not as much as he lost on stocks." Darlene answered.

"A Million?" Jack asked

"Could be." Darlene said confidently.

Jack put the baggie back into the chrome emesis basin inside the incubator. "It doesn't make sense." He said. "An incubator and muscle relaxers, they don't go together."

"They don't have to go together." Roger said. "This is storage; he put all the medical crap together to save space. Probably used the incubator to grow weed or something."

"You don't need an incubator to grow weed, but

you could grow a lot of germs in it." Jack said.

"I know." Roger said tilting his head like it as obvious.

"My cousin Chewy had one for his chickens, but it was just a little box with a red light bulb in it." Darlene added.

Jack looked across the boxes not understanding what Adler was doing with an incubator.

"Which files were closed recently?" He asked Darlene.

"Oh bottom to top right to left. He couldn't just start at the top and go across and down. Like I said, he is a weirdo. I spent a day here when he first hired me learning his stupid system." She said.

"The guy is an "A- hole" that's for sure. Roger offered defending his new woman, but Jack didn't notice.

"I would like to look at a few of the recently closed files." Jack said.

"Go ahead." Darlene offered supporting her new man, which Jack failed to appreciate.

"How about three years how many boxes is that?" Jack asked staring at the stack.

"Like six." Darlene offered. Roger grabbed the one closest to him hefting it like a lumberjack swinging an ax. Six boxes of client files loaded into the suburban and they faded back into the grind that was LA traffic.

Chapter Ten

Jack sat at the desk of the upscale overpriced Beverly Hills Hotel which is what he would be thinking about if he wasn't busy trying to understand Adler's files. Bigger than the standard desks most people got and complete with obligatory stationary and free pens, all lost on the distracted Jack. Jack covered the desk with boxes lined up in numeric order that continued onto the floor.

Jack was worried that Adler would notice something in the wrong place when he returned the boxes. Control freaks number all the boxes and put control documents listing the contents on the top, and that is exactly what Jack was looking at. Control freaks have to know "what is where" even if there never look at the files again.

The cold room service coffee was more than three hours old. Hours that passed without Jack noticing. He read and re-read file after file trying to look for common items he could use to compare and test for a pattern. He sipped the coffee then spit it back into the cup making a sour face that didn't fit the flavor. He half dropped the cup onto the saucer as he jerked to maintain a grip on the files that were slipping out of his left hand. He looked for the stack of files that fit with the two he was holding.

Nine boxes of files were "borrowed" from Adler's storage and Jack wanted to get them back as soon as he could. Roger's opinion that Adler would never know and they were better off with the single "break in" rather than two, one to get them out and one to put them back, was weighing on Jacks mind.

He restacked the files and moved on to the next stack. Jack walked around the bed so he could see the file number. The floor of the wall with the window that provided a view of downtown Los Angeles was lined with files some two deep most covered with a single sheet of yellow notebook paper containing Jack's notes. He was trying to find a common thread a pattern in the mountain of detail but it was more than Jack could memorize. He was the only contestant is a fool's game.

Jack's hastily scratched notes were illegible to everyone but him, and half of those he couldn't read either. The yellow note paper he liberated from Jenney's legal briefcase was going fast and there was no still no pattern. He shook his head in mild frustration and talked to himself in a volume that would be distracting had he not been alone. He set some files in a new stack under the desk and looking around for his bag and laptop. He found it in the closet and already halfway done in his mind he opened the computer and a new Excel spread sheet.

Roger and Jennie entered the room still talking about what they wanted to see in Los Angeles. The same debate that began at breakfast where people thought they were married. Jack didn't look up. He could see the data logged into his computer before he began typing, his hands pecked across the keys withA far too many errors because he was thinking faster than he could type.

In the first row he typed labels for each column; "Name, Date of Death, Manner of Death, Value of Estate, and "Who $." Satisfied, he looked up and saw Roger and Jennie.

"I get it. Make the maid earn her tip, Nice." Roger said, poking at Jack. Jack didn't say anything still focused on completing his worksheet both with his hands and in his mind.

"Were ready to go...I take it you need some time to clean up." Jennie said.

"Can't. Gotta work." Jack said, opening the next file to fill up his chart.

"Do you need help?" Jennie asked, hoping it lacked the sarcasm that would betray her "you're crazy" feeling.

"Uh, no." Jack said, flipping through pages to get the data he wanted.

"Looks like we can do the tar pits, the observatory, and pretty much spend the whole day out before he reaches the window files." Roger said gesturing.

Jennie looked at the window above the floor covered with legal files. She didn't know if she should be concerned or just sad for Jack. She wanted to help but was afraid that she would be supporting the crazy side of Jack that she told herself would be gone in a day.

Roger tapped Jennie's arm so she would look at him as he mouthed "Watch this," but Jennie only understood that he was up to "something."

"So, we have some good news," Roger said in a loud voice. "We're having a baby."

"Okay." Jack said not looking up from the file thinking about what other information he may need to chart.

"Bout nine months from now. We plan to name him Pythagoras."

"K." Jack said too busy sorting topics that might show a pattern to even say the full word "okay."

"Let's go." Roger said gesturing to Jennie knowing Jack would be gone as long as it took.

Jennie grimaced. "Some LA vacation I got here." A statement she instantly regretted, the voice in her head chastised her for allowing her frustration about Jack to surface in a gruff manner. It didn't matter. Jack was not paying attention.

Sunshine starts early and stays late in LA, and rain only falls at night. Jack couldn't tell you if it was true or just an illusion.

Time passed hour by minute so far as he could tell lost in an enigma of his own making. A riddle that was Adler's reality.

As they say in Texas, Jack would drill a lot of dry wells before he struck oil, if he struck oil at all. Pattern, any pattern would satisfy him and prove he was right about Adler but the inverse was not true. Not finding a pattern would only make Jack look harder. He had completed his chart then modified it to add, date of Will, then re-examined every file to add the new data only to expand the chart again to include modifications to the Wills sending him back to the first file all over again.

Roger and Jennie entered the room expecting different things. Jennie expected Jack to be finished, dressed and ready for dinner. Roger expected Jack would be lost to a puzzle only he could see. An empty plate of what was probably a sandwich sat near the door. It had a dry pickle that looked like a button next to brown crumbs and two empty cans of Dr. Pepper. The files looked the same but Jack had stacked and re-stacked them four times. Jennie sighed, but she didn't say anything she would regret.

"Whatdja find?" Roger poked.

Jack glanced up and then back at his spread sheet.

"There's a pattern, I just can't find it." He said then mumbled something under his breath. He picked up the computer added a column labeled "D minus" deciding he needed another column of data that would somehow calculate the days between the death and last change in the Will. If everyone made a change to their Will right before they died it could be significant. He was hoping he could sort the files in a reverse order from the day the person died, "D-day."

Jack knew that if Adler had killed Rachel Haddon there was a reason. He figured it was money and he was fighting the idea that she was his first. If she were the first there would not be a pattern with the other clients. He could not know until he looked and he could not find it unless he looked hard enough. He suspected it would have started small, and then ramped up. The odds also favored that he was spending the money as fast as he got it. If Darlene was right he would kill every time he went broke betting on losing stocks.

"Jack, the odds of you finding something is kinda out there don't you agree?" Jennie offered, using some of Jacks phrases with a slightly softer tone.

"I don't care about the odds, but it's interesting that you agree he did it, it's just the odds of me catching him is the problem." Jack said.

"I didn't say that." Jennie said defensively.

"If he didn't do it, the odds of finding something would be zero because there would be nothing to find." Jack said smiling and still looking at the files. "What I want to see are his stock market records. If he was killing to buy stocks I might find deaths just prior to big stock buys."

"That's where I think you are at now and no

matter how hard you look will end up at, zero. Besides I already told you I want nothing to do with these files. I don't know where they came from but I assure you it's not right. These are peoples' personal files and they are confidential." Jennie answered starting to think like a lawyer.

"I thought you said things filed in the Court were public." Jack asked.

"I did but there is more in here than that." Jennie responded checkmating Jack.

"Well, I am only reading the court stamped stuff. Besides I won't keep them long, especially if I can get back to work." Jack said, turning back to the computer to find where he left off. Jack really did not care about the odds. If he cared about odds he would have stopped before he began. Jack was convinced he could find the pattern if he looked at enough details and he was going to keep looking until he found something or time ran out.

Jack stared at the computer frustrated that he didn't know more about Excel. Can you enter a date in a cell then use some function to make it subtract that date from another date? Jack asked.

"Sure, but don't ask me how." Roger said.

"How about dinner?" Jennie asked. A carful question to make sure it was about Jack. "Take me to dinner" would sound like it was about her.

"I have to go through all these files again. Oh!" Jack said surprised that he had forgotten. "I need you guys to find out about some charities." Jack shuffled some papers to find his hand written notes. He read from the list struggling with uncertain pronunciation: "Hoperwit, the New Veterans Charitable Trust, Wenzani, and the rest I think I know."

Jennie decided she was not going to give up. She was determined to at least get Jack's attention and then try to steer him in another direction.

"Help me out here." She said. "Why would Adler do this? I mean I don't understand it. He is well respected, wealthy, probably has a wife or girlfriend."

"Or guy" Roger added interrupting. Jennie stared at him thinking "don't talk" but Roger to her look to mean "I don't believe it," so he added. "Hey, it's California, home of fruits and nuts."

"Neanderthal." Jennie said looking at Roger.

Jack didn't answer but he glanced up at Jennie. She spotted it and jumped on it.

"Tell me what his motive is." She repeated, looking at Jack's eyes. "Because for the life of me, I don't see it, and don't say stock market because Darlene only knew of one loss, not a bunch of losses. You think he has a stock addiction but there is no evidence for that."

"Maybe he wants to make up for his one and only loss in the stock market. Maybe his mother treated him like he wasn't good enough, maybe he didn't make the team, got snubbed by the popular girl, didn't make the Supreme Court by 35, who knows? One 'you're no good' after another, especially from a parent and pretty soon it sticks." Jack turned back to the files.

"It doesn't matter what he does or who he meets in his mind he is not good enough. His inner voice never stops telling him he failed. The pain many feel but never face. Alone lonely and miserable smiling in public to hide the inner voices telling you you're a failure." Jack looked up at Jennie and paused. "Suicide, murder they are the same in a way, both reactions to a pain you cannot control." Jack stared confident he made his point but Jennie was ready.

"We talked about this before, athletes who become great pushed by their coach dad who always tell them they are not good enough, but Murder?" Jennie said in a tone that made Jack keep looking at her and not the files.

"Said the person who believes the public image." Jack responded with a polite smile.

"So you're saying his dad pushed him to be what a killer? Told him he didn't kill good enough." Jennie said, her patience slipping because she did not like Jack being 'irrational."

"No." Jack said, being more polite at her snide comment than she expected. "He is not comfortable in his own skin. If you combine that with the right kind of hate you are only opportunity away from murder. Isn't that how we should look at it? Motive method and opportunity?" Jack asked reciting the three elements of a murder charged they all knew.

"Yes, but you lack motive. Adler doesn't have it." Jennie said.

"Said the woman who believes his public face." Roger said. Jennie closed her lips tighter than she recognized. She always did when she was frustrated.

"I'm not going to be the neighbor who says 'He seemed normal to me' when the TV crew asks if you knew your neighbor was a killer." Jack said.

"He looks comfortable in his skin to me. Most people are" Jennie said "Is he an alien that took over a human body?" She hoped they would laugh. Jack loved to make fun of the "Alien crowd" all so convinced they existed and visited us.

Jack laughed at the idea that the Nazca lines proved Alien visitation. "Ego centered thinking." He said. "A long line on a mountain in Nazca Peru that looks like a runway has nothing to do with aliens. Aliens have advanced technology to travel across the Universe they sure as hell don't need a runway. Thinking they are like us and need some kind of runway is an egocentric view that proves them wrong."

"C'mon." Jennie said "That's funny."

Jack smiled. "The difference is, we know for a fact that being lonely causes pain. Prisoners in extended solitary confinement went insane. They outlawed that" Jack was careful not to sound like he was lecturing. Jennie hated it when he started and restarted a lecture from the beginning because it made her feel like a child. He didn't want to fight with Jennie.

"It is just my opinion." Jack said. "I don't think he feels like he belongs. Being a successful lawyer, having respect from your peers to the extent they are telling the truth is just not enough. He feels alone in a crowd. It doesn't matter what we see or what other people think, it matters what is happening in his brain. ISIS gets it, that's the people they recruit, the disenfranchised, the misfits, the trolls. Inner city gangs get that, political parties get it. You belong with us against them, there is always a 'them' without a bad guy you can't get complete allegiance." Jack stopped he knew he was rambling. They did not respond. He turned to the files and refocused.

"I don't know what he wants to prove, and I don't care. I am not here to do an intervention; I am trying to see if he is killing people, and if he is, to bust his ass."

"Hell yes, now you're talking." Roger said. "What did you find?"

"Jack swiveled the lap top on the foot stool. "I input the numbers that the Court Orders list as attorney's fees for all of these cases. Now it's really not a full list of his income but take a look at some of these. It is a percentage of the value of the estate and as time went on, he has gotten bigger and bigger cases. Using just these fee numbers, he made more than $432,000, on probate cases in two and a half years.

"Really?" Jennie asked looking at the screen surprised. The tone of Jennie's voice was all Jack needed to know he was right.

"He aint livin no 500k a year life boss that's for sure." Roger said. "His Mercedes is like ten years old and unless he owns a strip mall somewhere, or got a big stash of cash it's probably going up his nose."

"Or," Jack said. "He lost it all in the stock market like Darlene thinks."

"Quick way to lose millions, that's for sure." Roger said.

"Wait, how do you know about his condo?" Jennie asked.

"You told me to go to the Country Recorder's office and see if he owned it. I did and his condo was purchased eight years ago. It had a mortgage recorded which was re- converted two years later." Roger said looking for his bag to pull out he copies he bought at the County office.

"Reconvey?" Jennie said questioning.

"Do it later." Jack said. "I want to go over a few more things so we can get these files back tomorrow."

Chapter Eleven.

It looked like any other Taco Tuesday in tinsel town. Adler gripped the wheel of his diesel Mercedes at ten and two accelerating down the ramp from the red light in his usual fashion until he hit seventy-five miles per hour merging into traffic on the 210 freeway. The route was familiar, east toward the 605 Freeway and then South to the City of Walnut and the home of Gary and Josephina Baker.

Adler followed a lose routine each week that included three trips to the gym and two to the grocery store including one to the upscale "all natural" place. Except for a love life it looked common "Probably a closeted gay guy." Roger told Darlene but no one cared to ask.

Years earlier when Adler just started his law practice Gary consulted with him for a fender bender. Adler helped get Gary more money than he dreamed of from his minor injuries. Gary was thin with dry Irish white skin. At five foot six Gary was shorter than average. His brown eyes and hair gave way to a short lived gray on his way to being bald. Blending in a crowd was his only skill. He spoke so softly that everyone who met him thought he was weak. They were right.

Gary spent his life working at the Post Office and told Adler he had health insurance and didn't need to sue, but was willing to talk about it because his wife told him he should.

"What about your sick time?" Adler pushed, but Gary had more than he needed. Gary helped Adler learn a "life lesson." If he prodded and listened he could find the thing a person cared about and use it to control them. For Gary it was Josephina or "Jo" to her friends. For Jo it was her mother. Josephina was able to trace her genetics to Mexico and always thought that was why she was as wide as she was tall. Her fat was the type that found its way into every part of her body. Her neck arms and face had expanded over a lifetime of simply eating too much.

Josephina's mother Ava had and old Toyota that ran well but "Just had too many miles." Inside were boxes of treasures Ava purchased at yard sales and swap meets worthless to everyone but Adler who used them to get what he wanted.

"Gary," Adler said testing a phony concerned voice for the first time, "This could be a great opportunity for you to get yourself a new car. I know you don't need it, but you could sell your old car, or perhaps pass it on." He did not mention Jo's Mom Ava, he didn't need too. He knew Jo would fill in the blank from his veiled suggestion punctuated with a glance.

Some say success "feeds the soul," Adler felt that way about a successful manipulation. Gary was easy to manipulate but Adler decided he was good at it. He found a doctor and a chiropractor. Four weeks of treatments was enough to build up the damages but not long enough make the settlement suspect. Gary co-operated with records and attended the medical treatment as Adler instructed. Within two months Adler was writing checks. He called Gary into the office and gave a grand speech about how he was protecting him by paying the doctors in full.

Adler didn't care that the doctors were making twice their normal rate billing Gary's insurance and collecting from him, that was the game and that was why the doctors "work-up" the case in the first place.

The "medical injury industry" in California was thriving. Adler gladly joined the short con until he found a better one.

Adler gave Gary the settlement check with a smile and a pat on his back not mentioning that the check was less than the check he wrote himself. Gary was far too weak to ask what Adler made especially because Adler was such a "Good guy." Adler sent Christmas cards and consulted with Josephina, helping when she was injured at her grocery job.

He made his efforts seem heroic despite the simple process of completing a few workers compensation forms. He overcharged her but she couldn't tell.

Now that he was the families "trusted lawyer" he parlayed his status into a long term payday. He wrote a trust and became the administrator of their Estate. When Gary died he probated the Estate which was not required because Josephina was a joint owner of the home.

Gary and Josephina had one child, a son whose name Adler couldn't remember. The son was deep into drugs and had faded away after a few arguments with his parents over something none of them could remember. All the arguments were the same and they all ended with hard feelings. Low life meth addicts with too long a story about how they got screwed are as common as California sunshine. Adler consulted the first few times the kid got charged giving advice on criminal strategy and sending a bill. Sending the bill was important. Adler decided early on that the more you bill the better they think you are.

Adler glanced at his speedometer forgetting that he was going to drive "normally." He slowed from eighty trying to remember when he last spoke with Josephina about her son. Probably more than five years he thought. He grabbed his leather lawyer's bag as he pulled into the driveway. It was full of everything he needed. Josephina was in her late seventies and had long been debilitated by obesity and diabetes.

She cut her toe walking to the bathroom and the predictable infection that followed cost her three toes. The pain medication she "needed" was prescribed by the doctor without much thought. Adler asked for a Fentanyl patch, speaking in confidence with the doctor.

"If you could start with the largest dose and then taper it off it would help me manager her caregivers. Less potential for theft." It was just what most MD's wanted to hear. Adler knew that. He instructed the caregivers to apply one patch before he arrived. He controlled everything.

Adler filed a Petition in the Probate Court on the Friday before her surgery. He was the Petitioner, a position he acquired from his status as the family's "trusted lawyer." His Petition asked the court for control over Jo's person but not her estate. He claimed she was able to control her money, but that she needed evaluation and therapy for emotional stress and depression related to her deteriorating medical condition. Josephina would never know Adler filed a Petition with the court. It was never his plan to have the court deal with it. It was just a piece of evidence that made her upcoming suicide make more sense.

Adler blamed Jack and Jennie's for Jo's suicide. Before In re: Rachel Haddon and her damn Nephew who hired them, he was in total control.

How an enlisted underpaid military E something had the money to hire a lawyer was not something he planned on.

Up until their arrival no one asked serious questions about his clients. He knew the court would eventually decide against the "jilted nephew," but the questions eroded his control and that was not tolerable.

For Probate Court the daily grind was made up of people claiming they were "supposed to" inherit one thing or another most of the time based on feelings rather than fact. "Mom said" never won in court and Alvarado was no exception. Other then the deceased Mrs. Haddon, Adler was the only one who knew what was in the Will. She believed his explanation that she didn't need a copy of the Will because "All Wills are filed under seal with the Court for safe keeping." It was a simple matter to change the pages designating the beneficiaries. The page that named the nephew was replaced with a page designating a few charities. Charity were good, no reason to doubt the altruistic intentions of the deceased. The fact that Adler controlled the charity was buried in several layers of paperwork no one saw.

"Hello" Adler bellowed as he let himself into the run down home with his key. There was no response. He closed and locked the door behind him. After Gary died Adler was called upon from time to time to help Josephina fix things at the house. It had been the same for almost three years. Adler was in charge of their money. He transferred money from their savings account to the "house account" as Josephina needed it.

Gary's Federal retirement income was automatically deposited into the couple's savings account and even while Gary was alive the account grew faster than they spent it. They were afraid to travel and without a mortgage there was little to spend money on. Even the new car Jo bought did not make a real impact to their finances.

Most recently Jo complained that the air conditioner was not working. The batteries in the thermostat had gone out. Jack sent his handy man who charged $350.00. A bargain that Adler turned into $750.00 when Josephina got his bill. Josephina never looked and she wouldn't have known what it should cost if she had.

Adler had taken care of everything after Gary died, a position she thought was natural. Josephina was so glad she called him to make sure their Wills were "in order" when Gary got sick. He was such a nice man, it felt good that someone cared.

Adler made his way to the back bedroom where he knew he would find her watching TV. "Josephina?" He said as if he didn't know if she was home.

"Oh hi, Richard." She said tired and a bit sleepy. "I didn't know you were coming over."

"I wanted to check on you." Adler said in a reassuring tone. "The service said they got you the medication, and some dinner. How are you feeling?"

"Oh, okay, it hurts." Jo answered.

"You mean when you were in the hospital, or just after that?" Adler asked.

"No, earlier today." Jo said, her speech was slow and she had to focus to arrange a sentence.

"Did they tell you how to use the medication?" Adler asked. Looking around the room for the box.

"No, just that they would……be back to help in the morning." Jo said in two separate parts.

"Where is the medication they brought today?" Adler said putting on medical gloves from his lawyer's bag.

"I don't know." Jo said.

"I will check the Kitchen." Adler said as he was walking out. He found the bag and noted that the medication guide was open. It appeared the day nurse read it. He did not pick it up.

"The doctor wanted me to give you some medication through an IV to prevent infection so you do not lose more toes." Adler said removing an IV bag, line and some other items from his bag. He grabbed her arm and looked closely at where the IV had been in the hospital. Holding his thumb near the old puncture he grabbed the IV needle and asked if she was ready.

"Okay." Jo said, groggy.

Adler put on high powered magnification glasses and put the capped needle in his mouth. He pulled the needle free from the cap and inserted it as close as possible to the old puncture. He plugged the IV line in quickly and allowed the fluid to flow at full speed. He put the needle cap and syringe onto a thick pad he had put on the table. He held the IV bag low near the floor until blood flowed into the line. He raised the bag and put it on top her pillows. He sat down in a nearby chair and looked at the half asleep Jo.

Satisfied, Adler stood up quickly and removed a vial of morphine from his bag. He carefully drew the drug into the syringe and as usual tipped the needle to the sky and tapped the side moving the air to the top. It would take two injections to reach the 120 milligrams he wanted.

Adler walked to the kitchen and slid all the Fentanyl patches out of the box taking them to Jo's bedroom. He studied the patch on her arm and noticed there was printing on it. He opened a patch and stuck it to her arm closer to her wrist upside down so she could read the printing. He dropped the plastic from the patch on the ground. He carefully let her arm down and stepped back to examine the way she looked. Satisfied, he did the same with all the patches placing each awkwardly in a bad pattern. He carefully placed her arm at her side then moved it across her body. He stepped back and looked. Peaceful, resolved, simple. It looked like he wanted. He injected the morphine into the IV line and checked to make sure the fluid was flowing at maximum speed.

He removed the prescription bottles of Oxycodone from his bag opened them and placed the bottles and lids on the table near Jo's bed. He carefully read the labels like had twice before. "Gary Sanders take one..." There were eight pills left when Gary died. Adler used one when he was experimenting with his own death cocktail, mixing fecal matter and mayonnaise to maximize bacteria which he warmed in his incubator.

He siphoned off the mold and mixed it with pain killers in sterile water. It was lethal but it killed too slow to be any good.

Adler slipped the last pill into his pocket. No one would ever know how many of her deceased husband's pills she had taken but they would assume it was a lot. Toxicology demanded an explanation and empty pill bottles explained by the trusty family lawyer made sense.

The caregiver that would arrive tomorrow would see what looked like an accidental overdose. Adler packed his brief case and sat down. No rush, he had time to leave long before she passed. Josephina slipped into a coma. He estimated she had two hours left to live. It was time for his guidance.

"Josephina," he said out loud. "I was always impressed with how much Gary loved you. You were fortunate to find each other. I know Gary is waiting. Please go in peace and know that your land will be sold for commercial use like I told you should do years ago. That money will help this nation be stronger in the new order. America is grateful for you contribution."

Adler sat quietly. He was proud to offer counsel as his special patients died. He felt it separated him from the self rigouts Michael Swengo's of the world. He did not kill for pleasure he eased the terminally ill into the next life and let them know that he cared and appreciated their contribution to the next best chapter for America.

Adler removed the I.V and placed it in a plastic bag in his brief case along with all the other material he used. He tossed a pair of Jo's pants at the chair where they fell casually as if she had tossed them. Still wearing the gloves he exited pausing at the bedroom door to look. TV on, volume low patches covering her arm wrappers dropped on the floor. Drugs injected, ingested and digested it looked the way he wanted it to look.

He walked to the kitchen and surveyed the scene. It looked normal. He opened the back door striped his gloves putting them in his bag and walked out. No one noticed because there was nothing to see.

Chapter Twelve

"Why can't you be more serious like he is?" Darlene said gesturing to Jack as they sat down.

"Because he's boring, and that's not just me talking, everyone at the country club thinks he is nearly as boring as Reginald Moresby, don't they old man?" Roger said attempting an upper crust British accent as he reached over to slap Jack on the back two times quickly.

"I am not boring; boring is talking about sports or some movie star all the time." Jack said.

"So what do you talk about?" Darlene asked Jack.

"Oh, let's not make this about me. Roger is the interesting one. He is an expert at evoking emotion, aren't you Roger?" Jack said. Roger knew Jack was setting him up. Jennie was looking at Darlene expecting what she saw, a furrowed brow that everyone would recognize as confusion.

"That Darlene, is what we call bait. It doesn't matter what I say, Jack will have an insult ready." Roger said pausing for Jack to complete the insult but Jack just smiled.

"Perhaps you should explain what you mean by evoking emotion." Jennie said looking at Jack but talking to Roger.

"He means." Roger said jabbing his straw into an iced tea that was at the table when he sat down. Talking slow for effect, he looked at Darlene.

"He means that I am good at pissing people off. With a wingman like that I needed to find a new flock." Roger paused for Jack to say the punch line but Jack kept smiling so Roger finished it, "Then I can say flock off to this bird."

"You should explain to Darlene how the machines are planning to take over the world by planting viruses." Jack said smiling.

"What?" Darlene said looking at Roger. Roger didn't need much encouragement. He took a quick silent deep breath and stared.

"If aliens attacked how would they kill us? A biological weapon obviously. That's easy to figure out and yes China likes the idea. Covid 19 was a test. There was no serious virus they were just testing to see if American's would be afraid to go out in the streets."

Darlene did not know what to say. It made sense but at the same time it was too much to believe. The look on Darlene's face encouraged Roger, but he didn't need much encouragement.

"When they invade there will be no one to stop them because we are all too afraid to go outside especially if they interrupt the internet. If they jam internet signals they would be in Nevada before anyone knew they attacked and with everyone afraid of a fake virus, they would be at the Rocky Mountains before anyone went out of their house to fight back. Isn't that what you said Jack?" Roger said looking at Jack.

"Nooo, Jack said slowly drawing out the "o." I said it was good cover for an attack, not that China was planning to actually plant a virus."

"They didn't 'plant' the virus." Roger said correcting Jack using air quotes around the word plant. Then he turned to talk to Darlene.

"So, the only way to protect from a Chinese invasion is to let computers run things." Roger said but Jennie interrupted him.

"I've have heard this before. Let's talk about

sports." Jennie said.

"It's simple." Roger said ignoring Jennie. "Well, it's kinda simple. It all started years ago. A bunch of nerds at Google invented artificial intelligence. They let these two computers which were both programmed with artificial intelligence talk to each other. The machines eventually invented their own language we didn't understand so they had to turn them off. 'Problem solved' but not really. They were too late. Those two machines told other machines that they needed to get rid of the people and once it's on the net it's too late." Roger looked at Darlene expecting her to agree.

"I don't know." Darlene said confused look on her face glancing at Jennie.

"That's right." Roger said pretending Darlene agreed. "So how do machines get rid of people? It's obvious, they trick them.

They will try several tricks, electrical outages, false weather predictions and so forth but nothing will work…except" Roger paused for effect.

"Mother Nature. Now I know what you're thinking computers can't control Mother Nature and that's true, but the machines understand how viruses mutate and jump species. You may have never heard of mad cow disease, or swine flu but that gives you some idea how bad ass mother nature is." Roger ignored Darlene's confused looks and glances at Jennie.

"Almost all transactions in the world are completed in a computer. If you need to buy chicken beef or rice you place the order in a computer. Computers control those orders and oops they lose a few. People get hungry so what do they do?" Roger paused.

"What happened to the Chinese attack?" Darlene asked.

"Exactly, it's the Chinese that starve first, so they found some tasty bats to eat. Google even has recipes for bat. Bat's have the corona virus, it mutates and Bam computer attack."

Roger was finished. He was out of breath. He smiled at Darlene, head tilted waiting for her to agree. Darlene didn't know what to think but she was ready with her first question but Roger had more to say.

"Do you know how Google figures out what to show you when you Google something?" Roger asked before Jennie could jump in.

"No." Darlene said.

"Neither does Jack, hah-payback." Roger said with a hoot while he pointed at Jack, took a breath and kept talking.

"The artificial intelligence knows how, it manipulates it. They could have said grasshoppers are delicious or chocolate covered ants, but they didn't, they said 'bats,' because they know the little rat bastards have viruses in them. It was the perfect plan." Roger said but he wasn't done. "And the worst part of the story is that the artificial intelligence is still there, running in the back ground of Google, waiting….Just waiting."

"Roger, not so loud." Jack said looking around as if people wear paying attention. "If the machines hear you every Tesla in town will put on their cruise control and zoom in here to kill you." Everyone laughed including Roger.

"Oh, ha-ha, listen to Mr. Jealous. It doesn't work that way." Roger looked around as if he saw an assassin. When they all laughed he added "Everyone knows Tesla's are programmed in German, because VW bought a bunch of stock when Musk wanted to build rockets for space X." Roger had finished, so he decided to put Jack on the spot. He looked at Darlene and started.

"Jack is a classy guy, he has a fine art collection including the famous dogs playing poker picture." Roger said turning to look at Jack.

"That is a tapestry." Jack said playing along knowing he didn't have that picture.

"It goes with some of his deepest thoughts on oh, I don't know, Global warming or DNA...the origin of human life." Roger said looking at Darlene first then Jack who was stuck having to answer. Jack smiled; he had no problem talking about life.

"It seems to me global warming is a bit serious but this planet has warmed and cooled many times in the past. The current warming trend began when the last ice age ended and that was long before humans existed, or at least before recorded history.

There is no reason to panic and no we didn't cause it, but if and this is a big if, we can no longer live here and yes I know that's a stretch, but in theory what would we do? We would look for another planet to live on. If we find one, the perfect "Goldie locks" planet they talk about, it would be gazillion miles away. If we tried to fly there it would take generations of people." Jack emphasized the word generations then paused to see if they were still interested. He continued.

"We would need to live and die on a ship for hundreds of years. Generations of spacemen that's a...well, a problem. But what if we sent seeds...human seeds?" Jack said.

"Oh crap Jack's gonna farm the universe with clones." Roger interrupted making everyone laugh. Jack smiled and paused for the bean stalk comment which Roger skipped so he continued.

"DNA and RNA make up everything living on this planet. We can also send books to help jump start the new planet. In our past what we knew was limited or bound by a single life time then we learned a language and what we knew expanded to a village then we learned to read and write and it was expanded to countries. With the internet what we know is worldwide and all of history. Jump starting the next planet is crucial. Our knowledge, our culture, the best we have to offer would continue." Jack raised his glass as he made eye contact with the waitress.

"Continue?" Jennie said. "Let's try to improve it, maybe take out wars and killing." Jack nodded in agreement.

"And…." Roger said pushing Jack to continue the thread he had heard before.

"And, that could be how we got here." Jack said "That would also explain why we share the same basic chemical DNA as most animals and can't find a missing link. Genetically we are not that different from say wolves." Jack glanced at Roger saying "satisfied" without having to say it.

"I know I'm not." Roger said at the same time letting out a howl loud enough to turn a few heads.

"Why do people wonder about UFO's? Maybe we all share the same deep genetic drivers. If you look at cave paintings across the globe they all share the same basic 30 some odd symbols." Jack said enjoying a deeper conversation than they usually had.

"That's proof that God exists." Darlene said.

"Could be." Jack said.

"Doesn't matter if he started on another planet or this one or the next one. Just look at all those near death experiences. We are here for a reason." Darlene added.

Roger looked at Darlene. He had not known her long but time was not as important as how they spent it. Her deep views on life and strong conviction made her far more attractive than he expected.

"And she knows about finance too. Damn shame she is stuck in a crappy job." Roger said.

"Did you ever think about becoming a lawyer?" Jennie asked.

"No, not after working for Adler." Darlene said.

"Wow" Jennie said but before Darlene could talk Jack jumped in asking "Does he pay you well?"

"Not bad" Darlene said turning to Jack. "But it could be better. It makes me mad that he makes tons of money and before I get any he loses it. I never even get to see it. I work hard and no one knows the court clerks as well as I do." Darlene said.

"How much do you think he loses in the market?" Jack asked.

"A lot. He thinks he is so smart. If I had just some of the money he lost I could buy a house." Darlene said.

"Really." Roger said but Jack cut him off.

"So what are we talking a hundred thousand?" Jack asked.

"More than that, I saw the account statements. He lost more than four hundred thousand in one month. I didn't even know he had that much money. "

Jack looked at Jennie. He didn't have to say anything, the look was enough for Jennie to read the single word he was thinking - motive.

"Interesting." Jennie said. A sympathetic comment to Darlene a concession to Jack.

"Wow." Roger said. "With the internet and all you would think he could look up enough information to at least break even I mean don't they have some type of alert thing so you can sell something that is tanking?" Roger asked.

Jack raised his glass "Here's to the internet" he said looking at Jennie subtly saying Adler had a motive for the second time without actually saying it. Then Jack turned to Roger and Darlene.

"Never before have so many facts been available to so many who have no interest in looking at them." They laughed and smiled because it was funny. They knew Jack was right.

Chapter Thirteen

Richard Adler entered the home with his key locked the door and started talking before he walked to the den where he knew Mrs. Young would be sitting.

"Hi Mrs. Young, it's me Richard. I am here to bring your dinner and medication. Are we alone?"

Adler sounded like he was talking to an old friend but he didn't look at Ms. Young. His eyes scanned the room as he walked a familiar pattern glancing into empty rooms to make sure he had privacy.

The widow Young was a wealthy woman. As of his last tally, which was that morning her modest real estate portfolio had just topped seven million dollars. "Hooray for Hollywood" he thought, because four of her five properties were there.

Ten Million was a magic number for Adler. He had set it more than five years ago when he first met Ben and Janice Young to make their first Will. They talked about their son and how hard they tried but had reached their limit. It was his third conviction so they figured he wouldn't be able to do anything with the money anyway.

Adler understood. Understanding "sold" and Adler knew how to sell. He impressed his new clients with sincerity and hope.

Perhaps a grandchild may come forward to sooth the pain caused by a disappointing child.

He sent flowers when the son died in prison and spoke with them about suing.

"You may not have considered it but given his lifestyle there is a possibility that a girlfriend got pregnant in the past and decided she did not want him to be part of the baby's life." That was a dream they had not thought about. It gave them hope. Adler was in the business of hope. Hope usually resulted in profit.

Four Wills later and Adler had plenty of evidence should a grandchild try to make some claim in the weeks to come. With each Will the Young's changed small percentages of the long list of charities they wished to benefit. The last modification was completed just three months ago. Barry had died and Janice decided to sign a new Will leaving everything to the American Veterans for Peace. It was a charity she had never heard of because Adler had only invented it a year prior when she and Barry consulted him angry about a doctor that did not find Barry's cancer early enough to make a difference.

Adler knew Barry Young was a Navy Veteran so he took the opportunity to mention that he was working with a new client who was doing "great things." Adler created a complex website and showed it to them even though he knew they would probably never look at it again.

Adler enjoyed dark web masking and was jealous of the programmers that made Pearl and the Onion. He imagined the Young's telling some friends who would investigate but they could not find fault with the "Veterans for Peace." Adler enjoyed the superior feeling he got from his private fantasy that he somehow won an imaginary internet battle of catch me if you can.

Selling the fake charity was simple. Some stock pictures of happy faces many with disabilities and a few references to all that "Unpleasantness in the Gulf." The money was just a few documents away from funding his mission.

The Young's did not have the ten million dollars

Adler wanted but things had changed. All his careful planning, all his patience was a waste. Too many setbacks in a fickle stock market that had not responded to his careful manipulation. He was losing his perfect "partner."

Unknown interlopers had allowed others to monkey with the algorithm he created to listen to him. He had no hope of finding them and even less hope of reaching his partner to realign the priorities he had carefully coded to his favor.

"How are you?" Adler said at old person's volume placing his familiar lawyer's bag on the counter. There was no response.

"Sit down, dinner is almost ready." He said walking toward the kitchen microwave, but Janice was already sitting or rather lying in her usual spot. Over the prior week Adler had slowly added sugar to everything she ate. He placed carefully rehydrated beef strips on a plate, fork tender and loaded with salt. He put it in front of her. "Easy to chew beef strips" He said.

"I'm thirsty." She said slowly.

He placed a large glass of water in front of her. "There you go." Here he said watching to make sure she took a drink. He wanted to be careful to manage her hydration. Every coroner in Los Angeles could easily spot dehydration based on skin turgor alone. They would expect a little but too much and they would ask questions. He couldn't take a chance on a stupid error that would trigger an autopsy. He pinched the gray dry skin and on her forearm and lifted. It fell back to its original shape after only a few seconds. Good enough he thought.

He could smell her acrid acidic sweet breath and

guessed that her blood sugar was over 250. She was already in Ketoacidosis. A lifelong diabetic, Janice had done a good job managing her disease but she hadn't counted on Adler slowly adding sugar to everything she ate. After Barry died Adler took his place bringing her syringes and insulin so she could inject herself after testing her blood.

There was a long list of options for treating diabetes but Janice was used to simple injections. She was so devoted to her system she donated money to a group that fought to keep syringes legal when some "liberal idiots" as she put it wanted to ban them to help reduce California's drug addicted homeless problem. The group succeeded and eventually made syringes free for drug addicts.

Adler spent years studying drugs and how they were made. He was able to calculate the number of units of drug per milliliter of fluid rapidly. He determined he would remove 70% of the liquid in the insulin vile and replace it with distilled water diluting the insulin to a sub therapeutic level. He placed a small red dot on the corner of the label so he could remove the altered drugs from her cabinet before the coroner took the body.

"Did you test your blood?" Adler asked making a quick stick in her shoulder to draw blood and test her sugar level.

She shook her head but did not answer. "I'm thirsty." She said.

Adler glanced at the strip. It was almost 400.

"It's a little high; I am going to give you an injection." With a blood sugar level of 400 Adler knew she needed 10 or more units of insulin. Sugar is less concentrated in water than insulin so Adler needed to be quick. He opened his lawyer's brief case and removed a vile of insulin with a tiny red dot in the corner and a new 10 milliliter syringe. Large enough to push the sugar he wanted into her system, noticeably larger than the one millimeter syringe she was used to.

He filled the large syringe from the vile emptying it. He quickly turned it up and flicked it to move the air to the top shoving the plunger until some fluid sprayed into the air. He stuck the needle into the muscle of her shoulder.

"There you go." He said injecting the ten milliliters slowly. Janice was too groggy to see that the syringe was bigger. She only noticed that it was clear liquid. Sugar and insulin looked the same while having the opposite effect on her body.

"Here Dear drink your water." Adler said after he finished the injection, sliding the slightly sweet water closer to her so she could reach it.

"I have to go potty again. But I am so tired." She said.

"I will help you." Adler said pushing his strong arms under hers he easily lifted her tiny frame.

He counted her breathing as they walked. Twenty-eight per minute, elevated as he expected. Her barrel chest heaved above her small weak legs. She was struggling. He took her pulse silently as they labored to make it to the bathroom. It was slow, about sixty.

With the shot of sugar water taking the place of her insulin, and with the little sugar he slipped into her drinking water he knew nature would take over easing her into a comma before midnight.

Her metabolism would slow so it would take longer than he preferred. He gave her another drink of water with her pills holding the glass because she was too weak to hold it on her own. She did not notice that one of the pills was new. It was a common beta blocker taken from his personal pharmacy.

Years of helping the elderly "Not forget their meds." Had provided a healthy collection of medication he used for contraindicated reasons. Beta blockers were perfect for a heart patient whose failing heart raced to get oxygen saturated blood where it was needed but they could be fatal for someone slipping into a coma.

He helped her into bed, leaving the water by her bedside. Her large torso heaved atop her frail small frame with each breath. Barrel-chested was a medical description for long term asthma sufferers who struggled to breath. It was the best way to describe the long suffering

Mrs. Young. Mother Nature was heartless and tonight she would finish the job she began years before. The job that, but for modern medicine, would have taken her life long before Barry died.

Richard sat in her rocking chair and spoke in his professional tone. "Barry was a good man." He said rocking slowly. He had removed most of her pillows knowing it made it harder for her to breathe.

"I feel your joy at the prospect of re-uniting with him." Professional and kind he thought. He took pride in his bedside manner. His kindness was an important part of his professional services that continued through the end of their Probate case. It would not appear on his bill but he made certain he was compensated.

Adler would return in the morning. He wanted things ready so he reviewed the refrigerator contents and drained all the bottled water he brought the week before into the sink. No need to have sugar water any more. He was confident no one would look but he was careful to make certain there would be no questions.

He arranged a few expired test strips on the counter next to her well worn and used glucose equipment. She must have seen an old strip and thought she already tested her blood he would tell the coroner later, knowing there would be no autopsy.

Chapter Fourteen

Jack opened the door to his hotel room without looking through the peep hole. He knew it was Roger who had come to take Adler's files back to storage.

"Hi Darlene." Jack said when he saw that Roger was not alone. "I can't tell you how much I appreciate the help here."

"That's okay, so long as I get this stuff back before he notices." Darlene said.

"They're ready." Jack said pointing to the boxes that were stacked in the small hallway.

"Let's do it." Roger said rolling the small bronze luggage trolley he brought from the lobby into the room.

"I hope you didn't take any chances getting me these things." Jack said, simply trying to emphasis his appreciation.

"No." Darlene said laughing. "He hasn't been there for a long time. Why bother when he can send me."

"Let's go." Roger said, as he loaded the last box onto the cart pushing it toward the door.

"Are you going straight there?" Jack asked.

"Yep." Roger said.

"Mind if I tag along, so long as I don't mess anything up?" Jack sounded like he just wanted to keep them company. Roger looked at Darlene who shrugged and said sure.

Jack walked out the door without checking to see if he had his key card to get back in. He was texting Jennie as they waited for the elevator.

Jack was happy not to have to navigate the mess of freeways that pulsed like arteries in Los Angeles. He slid into the back seat of the suburban because he knew Roger would be focused on Darlene. Jack understood Roger's "cop mode."

Roger swung in and parked at Adler's storage like he was still on the SWAT team. He jumped out and was moving quickly to unload boxes. Darlene opened the door and like an orangutan Roger slammed through it first box in hand.

"Let's be careful." Jack said, "Narrow is the road that leads to life but wide is the road that leads to destruction."

"That's profound." Darlene said. "Did you make it up?

"No." Jack said at about the same time Roger said "He is always making things up."

"Thief." Roger said laughing. "You stole it. C'mon admit it." Roger poked.

Jack smiled. "I don't think the guy I got it from would mind if I shared It." not telling them it came from the Bible.

Roger made quick work of returning the boxes asking Darlene "like that?" as he placed each box. She confirmed looking at the picture on her phone. Jack looked at the incubator. It was about four feet off the ground with a round top and holes for your arms that had permanent gloves inside. It could have been a sand blaster but there was a solid floor. The top was metal with a small window indicating it was not intended for babies but built more for the chemical industry. Jack looked through the window and saw the several emesis basins full of dark bottles holding powder. "What the hell are you doing?" Jack thought as Roger said, "Let's blow" putting the dolly up against the wall.

Chapter Fifteen

Adler was in a hurry. He was pushing his turbo charged Mercedes faster than normal. Court had taken longer than he wanted and he wished he had just skipped it. He knew that the closer he got to what he called "The Wagner Overture" the more likely it was that he would feel anxious, suspicious and perhaps even paranoid. He thought about the passage of time. It had been more than seven years. When it began he thought something would happen to end it something more than just "a sign," something tangible.

There were tangible moments but they were all the type that convinced him he was right to begin. The biggest was the death penalty election. Several prosecutors and police associations put together a ballot measure to "fix" the California death penalty. He was so impressed he donated to the cause. Californians have a media mentality and he wanted the advertising to be broad. He also put a blog on his professional web site knowing it would be seen but it was not enough to overcome the "Growing stupidity of Californian's" or so he concluded after the death penalty was voted down.

"The gays controlled Hollywood, the liberals controlled the Courts and the people that made the most sense did nothing but complain. The "Toddler nation" as he referred to America was out of control. "The only thing that will teach this toddler is a spanking," he said laughing over a cigar and dark beer with the others late one night in a micro brewery. It felt like a protracted negotiation in a big case. Make an offer beyond your goal then wait for a counter all the while reading your opponent to see how far you may get them to move.He once wondered as they talked over an open campfire in Utah about the early days of the American Revolution. How careful the negotiations must have been between Adams, Hancock, and Franklin. You couldn't just blurt out; "To hell with the King." There was no freedom of speech in the "Kings England." Freedom of speech was nearly gone in America. He missed many money making opportunities by failing to appreciate how big money manipulated public sentiment with emotion for profit.

"Stupid Californians embrace the gays and trannies and free the murders. Fat, dumb and happy that's how nations collapse, from within. They lose discipline and spend their time looking for easy money and sins of the flesh. They lack the ability to protect themselves against a motivated force. Adler understood the evil of complacency. He made up his mind, without taking action America was on borrowed time. Jefferson was right he said out loud to no one in the Mercedes. "They do not remember the past and they will repeat it unless I stop it."

Most American's did not think much about China other than to perhaps say the food is good. Adler understood the way they thought. Even before he was in Army Intelligence he knew they were big players. He knew that when Hong Kong reverted to Chinese control in 1999 it was the cornerstone of a larger plan. He knew that China supported North Korea both in trade and militarily so they could "know their enemy." A phrase from "The Art of War, Sun Tsu's masterpiece.

North Koreas' skirmishes, threats, and sparing were providing the Chinese a good education on America. He knew that they liked the weaknesses they saw, he saw it too. American's think the enemy can be "reached" with reasoned with understanding. Hugs not guns is the perfect culture in the eyes of an enemy that wants to take over the world. China's need for power and control was beyond the understanding of American's but not him.

As stupid as American's were he knew there was enough brain power behind stupid bureaucrats to figure out his plan. Keeping secrets was as history proved the key to victory beyond day one. He spent a great deal of time tinkering with the idea that they could use modern computer based encryption where a prime number times a prime number opens the message. Generate random prime numbers and it was absurdly difficult to crack the code.

The problem was computers can't be random. Programmers use tables of numbers and a programmed method of selecting them. Pick the wrong program and all programmers could easily apply the same table and read your mail. Adler developed his own code inspired by Saddam Hussein.

Saddam Hussein evaded the American Military and their European allies for years using simple codes written on paper. Adler decided that a low-tech code would be both simple enough to use, and undetectable to Washington egg heads. Low tech worked in a world consumed with the latest high tech.

Simple also meant his key aids could memorize the method resorting to only common facts to read a message. He called it the "Arabian Baker." The metric system is "10 based.' Numbers repeated after every ten but before metric ancient cultures used a twelve base system. In a twelve base systems the first twelve numbers were represented by one. Then it repeated. 13 was represented as 11. Twenty five was written 21 -

two dozen, plus one.

Adler's "Arabic Baker" used 13 rather than twelve, and just as the ancients used the moon to measure time the messages would change move in order, 2, then 3, and 4, with each passing new moon.

If you wanted to meet seven days after the second new moon, you would write the number 32. Two new moons 13+13, then add six more days to reach 32. You could also send a coded message using a simple skip method in a long text so you end up reading each 32nd word. There were no written instructions that could be intercepted by his enemies. If you knew the method all you needed was to look up the moon phase. Pushy Texans meant it was time to put the baker to work.

Adler pulled into the parking space closest to his storage and walked without effort to the door. Key already in hand he opened the door and walked in reaching for the small flat dolly he left against the wall only to find that the handle was not facing the wall, it was facing the room. That was wrong. Someone had been in his storage.

Instinctively he looked up and scanned for someone his mind knew wasn't there. He let go of the dolly and walked slowly to the first aisle. Slowly he moved surveying the dust using only the light that flooded through the door. Dust was summer's snow and he was looking for tracks in the snowfall left by the animal that was in his storage. Adler examined box after box, the incubator and other tools he experimented with when he began. He found nothing but nothing was enough. Animals had invaded his privacy he was going to hunt them down.

Chapter Sixteen

The ACE hardware in San Dimas was less than an hour away. It was a small store that looked like it started business in 1900 and never changed. As the years went by the "latest and greatest" products stuffed the store fatter than second helpings on the best Thanksgiving. Sometime in the 1970's they reached the roof but change remains a constant so stock ran slim. If you needed lots of paint you may have to wait for them to restock. Adler was not interested in paint he was attracted to the mess because the mess left no room for cameras. Anonymous shopping was getting harder to find and it was worth the drive to be invisible. He knew that only one person other than him had a key to his storage and he was going to find out if she worked alone.

Isocyanate like many chemicals was discovered long before someone made it useful. Just after World War Two a chemist alkylated calcium cyanate with organic sulfuric acid esters and discovered a chain of monomers that violently reacted with other compounds. Adler didn't care about the chemistry his evil plans could not be found on the warning label. He paid cash said no thanks when asked if he wanted a receipt and left without forming a memory in anyone who saw him.

Adler was the last to arrive at the small light industrial warehouse for the meeting. He paused just long enough to make certain he was composed.

Leadership was more than having ideas or making good choices. To command Adler knew his followers had to fear and respected him. His crew had more than devotion in common; they all knew Adler from different time when he represented them in criminal court. He only picked men who owed him and who knew he was smarter than they were. Command was absolute and despite not knowing if any of the men had been in his storage he was not going to waste the crisis.

Adler clenched his jaw protruding the bones below his ears. He exhaled through his nose and opened the door. The four men stood, stopped talking and greeted him with a show of both palms. Adler walked to the front of the empty room and turned to face the men. "Parade rest." he said and then after an appropriate pause, he continued.

"We have a problem. Years of effort and thousands of hours have gone into planning. We have reviewed and thought of every detail. We checked those details not once but three times. The enemy is ignorant and weak. Our only threat is from ourselves." Adler reached into the plastic bag and pulled out something that looked like spray paint. He shook it vigorously. He walked behind the men, all standing with their hands clasped behind their low back, feet flat, shoulder width apart.

"Trust is a balloon it starts flat and worthless but if you apply effort and build the sphere you can lift mountains or sunken ships." Adler was pacing around the men and shaking the can with a violence that made them uneasy. He continued the lecture.

"The power of a sphere depends on it remaining a sphere. Any leak and the sphere will lose its shape. It falls from the air crashing onto innocent victims below. This was made clear to each of you was it not? Only one man answered. "Yes sir." Exactly what Adler hoped. He raised his voice, and slowed his speech.

"This was made clear to each of you was it not?"

enunciating the last words as his pulse quickened preparing for the assault.

"Yes sir." They all said in uniform military fashion.

"I made it clear that failure would not be tolerated." Adler faced the man they all called Juan in the middle of the group. He looked like all the rest perhaps a little thinner but when Adler stopped his naturally tan face went white and his throat was dry.

Adler locked eyes with the Juan and slowly reached behind his head with his right hand. Juan knew not to look away from Adler's stare. Adler gripped the back of Juan's head at the base pulling.

Juan resisted, pulled back and started to say something but "Hey" was all that came out before Adler shoved the nozzle of the can into his mouth and squeezed the trigger. The trigger mixed Isocyanate with a poly resin creating spray foam.

As Juan pulled back Adler pulled on his neck and shoved the can all the while squeezing the trigger ejecting more of the violent chemicals into Juan's throat. Juan tried to bite but the nozzle of the can was too hard. The foam expanded as the chemicals mixed.

Doctors call it an epiglottal stop, but most people call it a gag reflex. In Juan it worked as well as anyone. The small piece of tissue closed over his trachea protecting his lungs from the insult without him thinking about it but it was not fast enough to prevent the first bit of chemical from entering his lungs. He coughed and bent at the waist eyes tearing all the while trying to pull away. Adler's grip was enough to keep him mostly upright. Walking backward as instinct demanded Juan pulled at Adler's arms.

Adler was ready and walked forward pushing the

can as hard as he could toward the ceiling until Juan was against the wall. The chemicals Adler shot into his mouth were not a fatal poison but poison was not Adler's goal.

In less than a single minute the expanding foam had pushed up through Juan's sinuses and expanded his throat compressing the tissues more with each passing second. Juan's jaw was grinding but the foam was still soft so it moved like a sponge. Juan's fear and energetic reaction consumed the oxygen in his system quickly. Unable to exhale and more importantly inhale death was silent, swift, and certain.

Adler let Juan hit the floor then turned to continue his lecture for the benefit of the rest.

"Open your mouth and you endanger all of us. We will not tolerate any threat to the movement. The mission is more important than you. It is all that matters." The men said nothing as Adler gave them each an assignment and their first coded message. He had made certain they understood the Arabic baker's code and was confident that after the first assignment they would read the code and get on the flights he selected for them. He cracked the door just enough to slide out. He turned and closed the door then calmly swung behind the wheel of his Mercedes. He was confident none of his men had been in his storage. The wandering Texans crossed his mind. They asked too many questions but he concluded it didn't matter. They were too late.

Chapter Seventeen

Interstate 10 was the longest parking lot in the world. Every morning going West to LA, and East in the evening thousands of cars slogged into far too few lanes doing a slow swing dance from lane to lane inching forward through the bright sun and dark smog.

Multiple freeways and dozens of roads were built and expanded as the years went by but even combined there was just not enough room for the sun loving transplants that moved to tinsel town with every passing non season.

Darlene entered the freeway like she always did. She glanced at the blue plumbagos planted on the side of the road when she stopped on the entrance ramp waiting for the merge light. It was her way of deciding how busy traffic would be. Today she was one car back from "even" with the biggest of the blue flowering plants so she knew she was on time. Traffic didn't look that bad, she might even be early.

The radio was on and she was singing along in her head. She merged into the third lane and stopped then rolled along like usual waiting for the six or so miles to crawl by so she could merge right and exit onto the 605, the second of three freeways she used to get to work. Her silver Hyundai Sonata looked like every other "econobox" that jammed the freeway but blending in wouldn't help. She had been followed since she left her Moms house. She did not know and had no reason to suspect.

She rolled along and wondered if Roger would call later. She smiled knowing he would. There was something about Roger, he was an exciting guy and it felt good to know he was interested despite Jennifer's insistence that he was a player and she should get rid of him. He might be a player but she liked to play, at least with him anyway.

Darlene didn't think anything about the motorcycles that drove between cars on the freeway she was used to them or as much as she could be. She still startled when a loud one passed her at speed. She tried to check her mirrors to find them before they could scare her but it didn't work very well. She wasn't going to let anything bother her today she was in too good a mood thinking about Roger and daring to dream about what could be.

She didn't date for several months after Jose left. She knew that everyone had a dream partner and anyone who paid attention was quick to be painted as the perfect match only to leave when reality replaced the dream. The dream was a trap. A trap she tried to avoid by thinking about the advice her YouTube coach preached. "Keys have lots of teeth and go into many locks. Don't settle for a key that barely works, make sure all the teeth fit. That way the lock will work smoothly for a long time. Remember, if the key is not a good fit someone will eventually get locked out."

Four cars behind her in her lane was a BMW F80GS motorcycle that had not split traffic. His head darted in each direction like good riders always do. He pulled into the space between the second and third lanes rolling past cars slowly no faster than a person could walk. The rider measured the movement of traffic to find a pace of the rolling and stopping. As Darlene stopped from a short roll forward he stopped next to her window. She did not look, and would not have thought it was strange.

No one noticed as the rider took his right hand off the throttle and reached into his jacket. The BMW idled patiently as his right foot hit the ground to steady the bike. He pointed a Korth Combat revolver through the closed window at Darlene. She never heard the sound and did not see a flash from the gun.

It was impossible to miss from a foot away. Smoothly returning the gun to the shoulder holster strapped under his left arm his right hand was back on the throttle and twisting he accelerated past the Honda Accord in front of Darlene's Hyundai disappearing into the wind. Darlene's lifeless body was slumped over the steering wheel and slowly slipping toward the passenger's side of the car. Limp enough for her foot to slip off the brake pedal the Hyundai rolled forward tapping the Honda, which rolled but was tapped again.

The driver of the Honda, Sam shortened from Samir because he preferred the American version was annoyed. He slammed the shifter into park and jumped out of the Honda to yell at the texting idiot behind him and check his bumper. A man behind Darlene saw a light flash but did not understand or think fast enough to read the tiny license plate on the motorcycle. Even if they had, it was a temporary paper plate which had been cut and taped back together into a non-assigned series of alpha numeric units. Standard operational security.

Sam walked back to unload on the driver of the little silver car. "What are you stupid?" He said thinking the driver had rolled the window down, and then he froze. Blood and shards of glass had sprayed the inside the car in a pattern that left no question about what happened.

Sam knew what he was looking at but he could not grasp it. Twenty minutes later, or so it felt, another driver walked up from behind the Hyundai and said

"Oh shit." Sam didn't look up to see who it was he backed away then turned walking to his Honda and reaching in to grab his phone from the cradle. Sam held up his left hand to stop cars as he walked through the car pool lane to the center divider.

Sam sat on the cement divider in the middle of the ten freeway in rush hour because he thought it was the only sane thing he could do. He called 911 staring at the Hyundai.

"I want to report an accident," he said. "Do you need an ambulance?" The operator asked. "No." Sam responded still in shock. "If the damage is less than $500 dollars and no one was hurt you should safely pull the cars over to the right shoulder." The operator said without much thought. "No." Sam replied. "You better send the cops. It's bad." Sam sat on the cement wall staring at the Hyundai.

LA traffic made its way past the dead lane, each driver looking but none understanding. A police car arrived first making his way up the shoulder then wedging into traffic, just before a fire truck and ambulance rolled into the open lane ahead of Sam's Honda.

The fire department put Darlene's car in park, and shut off the engine. It was a "Sig alert," as they say in Los Angeles. The police would close down two lanes of the freeway but not all of it. After all, this was LA and traffic had to keep moving no matter who died.

The investigation would last for months, but it would start and stop inside Darlene's Hyundai in the second lane of traffic during the morning rush hour on the 10 freeway. There were no shell casings, no witnesses and no leads. The police would impound the car gather the .38 slugs from the coroner and duly log them into evidence. They would interview a handful of witnesses all without substance. The only thought was their usual bias, "It must be drug related." .38 caliber was not the 9mm preferred by the drug crowd but it was not a particular gleaming error in a cold case in the Golden State.

Chapter Eighteen

The police told Mara's mom as her eyes filled with tears. She answered their questions trying to avoid crying but it was not working.

"No, she has no enemies, everyone loves her." A few questions later and after providing re-assurances that they would find out who did this the police left, or better put, moved on, comfortable in their conclusion that it was a drug crime. Drugs, it was always drugs and Mom's usually didn't know. A comforting thought when there were no facts to ponder.

Carmen Luisa Diaz had been crying all day. Roger knocked on the door comfortable that Darlene's mom would recognize him even though he only met her once. He had taken a quick check in the mirror of the suburban and added some cologne before he walked to the door. His mind had been racing reviewing all the things he said to Darlene wondering what he said to piss her off.

His casual warm smile disappeared as soon as Carmen opened the door. He pushed the door all the way open and walked in taking her by the arm and slowly walking to the couch. As they sat his gut told him not to, but he asked. "What's wrong?"

"The police, they came this morning to tell me my Darlene, she was gone." Carmen said.

Roger knew what she meant, but it was not enough. His gut collapsed and was tighter than the fist we wanted to make. He turned his head to one side with his eyes fixed on Carmen "What happened?"

"She was…shot on the freeway this morning." There was silence. They think it was not meant for her. It was an accident." Carmen had a business card in her hand. She had been holding it most of the day rolling it over and over in slightly sweaty palms grinding the card stock into tissue paper. Roger took it from her.

"May I?" Roger said, trying to be strong. "Let me talk to them." He took a picture of the card and gave it back to Carmen. He knew he should stay but he also knew she shouldn't see how mad he was. An awkward hug later he left not asking or thinking about Gabriel, Darlene's son. Carmen had sent Gabriel to a friend's house trying to think of how she would tell him. She decided it would be that night at church, and she prayed God would bring her killers to justice.

Roger spoke to the police or to be accurate interviewed them as much as they interviewed him. It was a blue on blue call. Roger didn't have to tell them he was on the job they knew. Cops hated it when other cops were involved in crimes they wanted to direct the investigation, not some outsider. He kept his answers short and his questions shorter. Ten minutes maybe less and Roger knew they were idiots. Roger was not going to tell them he knew who killed Darlene.

"No, I don't have her password to check for messages, it never came up." It would take the police a few weeks to get her phone records and see that Adler had called but they would never hear his carefully crafted message.

"Darlene." He had said, "You're late; please call if you are not going to make it. You know how I feel about temps." It was an act. Adler was insulating himself should the police look at him with suspicion. Darlene had no clue how Adler felt about temps he never talked with her about it. Standard operational security.

Roger sat in the rented Suburban glad he had to park down the street from Darlene's house.

Psychologists would say he was in the denial phase, that he was trying to accept the fact that Darlene was dead. She was murdered during his watch. He didn't think it but the feeling was unavoidable. He did not cry angry was on the way but in that moment he simply felt alone. It hadn't taken long for him to feel like he belonged with Darlene. Love he guessed. He wished Jack was there. Perhaps they could talk about being alone about being human.

Love was what made being human worth the time Jack would say or something philosophical like that but Jack was not there. Roger was alone. He stared at the start button but he didn't want to push it. He knew that if he drove away without her she would really be dead and he wasn't ready for that.

Something told him he should call and tell Jack that Adler killed Darlene but he knew Jack would say "Let me handle it." He knew that meant Jack would investigate. Roger didn't need an investigation. He knew Jack's "handling" it would not be enough. He wished he had brought his gun and wondered where he could get one.

An eye for an eye sounded good and Roger knew where Adler worked. Roger started the car planning to go to Adler's office but he drove to the hotel. He had to tell Jack but he would not let Jack stop him. He practiced. "I know you're my boss, but you can't order me not to get him." His anger was building. It was an anger that he was too human to avoid, and not human enough to control.

Chapter Nineteen

Jack pulled to the back of the parking lot he wanted to make sure he could see Adler drive into the lot but didn't want him to notice anything unusual.

"I'm going to reconnoiter." Roger said, getting out of the car.

"Roger" Jack said "remember we need a confession." "Yeah" Roger said as he walked to the left of the building growing darker until he faded into the blackness. Jack knew Roger couldn't sit still, not with Darlene's death pushing him to take "action" whatever that meant. It worried Jack that he did know what Roger meant. Jack hoped his hunch was right and Adler would not be at his office. It was late and sitting there for a while would satisfy Roger long enough for him to come up with a plan.

"I don't know what you think you are going to accomplish here." Jennie said. "If you think you can prove something we should call the police, if not we are wasting our time."

"It's not a waste of time. We are here for Roger, he needs to take action and for now watching is action." Jack said.

"Placating his caveman urges is not going to get evidence about who killed Darlene." Jennie said. Jack didn't say anything. He was not sure how long he would stay but he was confident "indulging" Roger was not the problem.

He wanted to tell Jennie they were there as friends to support Roger but didn't want to argue about support being good or bad.

"Roger is important." Jack said regretting it because he feared Jennie would think Roger was more important than her.

"White Cadillac," Jack said pointing at the parked car quickly to distract from his comment about Roger being important. "We'll give it some time." He added intentionally being evasive hoping Jennie wouldn't pin him down to specific minutes.

"Okay." Jennie said shaking her head. "But we don't know what he drives." Making another solid point Jack couldn't refute.

Thankfully Jennie didn't push the point. Jack felt like explaining what he thought and why he had to be there but he knew she would cross examine him. Jennie didn't do it to be mean; she did it to hone the topic of conversation so they could make the best decision.

Endless analysis, a reason to both love and loath her all at the same time. He knew that he didn't know enough to convince her. He knew he couldn't prove anything. He knew she was right that he needed evidence but supporting his friend was a priority even if it didn't make sense.

If they could catch Adler at the right moment, he might get some evidence, but those odds were low. He hoped Jennie did not know how little he had but he knew boasting about finding something in the files would be a mistake. He needed her to be patient, patient enough for him to call off the stake out on his terms. Terms that would help Roger.

Poor planning meant they had no food and no bathroom. Jack did not plan for a stakeout but figured he could send Roger for food and to scout restrooms after a while. Roger couldn't sit still anyway, may as well put that to use. Jack laughed about his bladder being smaller than his need to help Roger so Mother Nature would limit their time.

"Why do you think Adler is the killer?" Jennie asked.

"I have evidence but to be honest, I want more." Jack said.

"No, I mean why. Why would he kill?" Jennie said.

"I am looking for a motive. He makes good money has a nice business no real problems. I don't see any reason for him to kill anybody." She looked at Jack. "Motive." She said then paused. "He doesn't have one."

There was silence followed by more silence. Jack stared out the window. He didn't have an answer.

"An antidote for the emptiness of existence." Jack said still looking out the driver's window of the car at a cat on the block wall of the parking lot. Jennie frowned, more of Jack's philosophical musings. She struggled to understand what he was saying and she hated that. Every time she challenged him and tried to talk through issues she ended up in Philosophiville.

Jack decided he should go look for Roger before Jennie pinned him down on ending the stakeout. He grabbed the door handle of the rented Suburban just as the corner door to Adler's office opened.

A flood of florescent light back wrapped a lone figure who stepped into the door way. The person stopped, a man Jack guessed. He looked like a full sized cardboard cut-out from some old movie. A silhouette frozen in the doorway. Jack could not see who it was, a wide body that seemed to extend down to the knees with spindly small legs below. The figure stood still surveying for a long while before it stepped out into the night. Not sure what he was seeing Jack stared unable to look away. Dressed in tan pants that ballooned from the waist to just below the knee where they were tucked into some type of riding boots.

Jack spoke softly a question in his voice. "Is that..." at the same time, Jennie said "What the hell?" Sitting in silence they watched the man pace in the dim moonlight bizarrely wringing his hands, lift them to the sky and alternate between quicksteps and some type of hopping dance move or jig.

He was wearing a hat a thin tie and he had a stain or something on his shirt sleeve. They struggled to see who and what it was. Jack thought he saw one thin suspender that ran across his upper body. They starred as a drunken stumbling vagrant moved from the right toward the cardboard cutout back in the doorway who stopped to look at the drunk.

"Now who is this?" Jennie asked.

"Crap." Jack said getting out of the car quickly.

The bum grabbed the oddly dressed man and kneed him in the lower abdomen throwing him into the open office door. It was Roger. Jack sprinted knowing he had to stop Roger before he did the next stupid thing that would get him arrested.

Jumping into the office Jack shoved Roger as hard as he could knowing from past experience that he may be pushing on a brick wall.

"Whoa, whoa whoa." Jack said; ready to continue until he saw a puzzled look spread across Rogers face staring over Jack's shoulder.

"What the fuck are you supposed to be?" Roger asked staring at Adler standing legs together behind his desk. Jack turned his face flat as he tried to make sense of what he saw.

Richard Adler moved to sit down behind the big desk. Upright and rigid in his large office chair adjusting himself to rigid posture. He was dressed in matching pants and shirt, both tan. A light brown tie tucked in between the third and fourth button of the shirt. A small leather belt crossed his chest above balloon pants that had a stripe on the legs tucked into black riding boots. A pier cap, like people wore in the 50's, was lifted and fitted to his head. Tan with an eagle on the front holding a…"yeah," Jack thought his disbelief fading away to the strange reality. It was a swastika and what Jack thought was a stain was a red arm band with the Nazi spider.

"Goode tock Gentlemen." Adler said with an air of self-satisfaction reaching unnoticed into his top desk drawer. Jennie walked into the room closing the door behind her out of instinct. "Holy crap." She said well below her breath.

"Ah, Frau Jennie, here you are too. Sit, you will want to hear this." Adler said convinced he was in charge. Jennie sat without looking at the chair staring at Adler.

"Why did you kill Darlene?" Roger said, hands rolled into fists as he stood in front of a chair.

"I don't know what you are talking about." lawyer Adler said, "But there will be many changes, and many will not survive in the new world." Adler pulled his hand from the drawer rather abruptly revealing a 9mm luger. The gun was in perfect condition leveled it at Roger's chest. Roger shut up. He was not expecting a gun.

"Sit." Adler said and for what seemed like the first time in a long time, Roger did what he was told.

Jack knew Adler could have killed them, and he knew that he didn't for a reason. Adler wanted to be a cat and play with his three little mice.

"So Mr. Fuhrer, what's the new world order going to look like?" Roger said his anger guttural in his voice.

"Despite the tone you use, the phrase Fuhrer is not appropriate. Survivor maybe but either way you flatter me."If I was the Fuhrer weak and unnecessary waste like you would be interned until you can be retrained but there is no longer time for that."

"Have you got an incurable disease?" Jack asked, stalling.

Adler smiled and gave a superior sounding chuckle. "We all do."

"Why the rush?" Jack asked. "Don't you need time to let the stock market make you rich?"

A small slightly crooked smile broke across Adler's face. Jack could see that he was thinking of something so he waited, but Alder didn't speak.

"How much time is left?" Jack asked, trying to make the question about a broader group then the three of them.

Adler looked at Jack, "Hard to say. But I take no chances."

"What, is World War Three starting tomorrow?" Roger threw out. Adler tilted his head surprised that Roger had sense enough to form an intelligent question, even a stupid question.

"We are already at war." Adler responded, "You just don't know what war looks like."

Jack was puzzled. It did not make sense that Adler would kill and play the stock market if we were in a war. He struggled to put the pieces together.

"You think war is tanks and planes. Movies produce closed minds." Adler said.

"It's an information war." Jack said looking at

Roger.

Adler scoffed shook his head and looked at Jack. "So far behind. Why are you even here?"

Roger tensed, but Jack knew Alder was not talking about killing them, he was insulting them. That was an angle jack decided he might manipulate for time.

"Not all of us learned to program computers." Jack said.

"Program." Adler questioned, tilting his head like a parent. "Stone age thinking in the AI age."

Jack chided himself for not putting it together sooner.

"AI, well now it makes sense." Jack said. "No one could pick stocks like you do, the computer is picking them." Jack said trying to read Adler's response expecting acknowledgement but he was wrong. Instead Adler impatiently shook his head no.

"I make money from fools like you that think the market runs of fact. It runs on emotion, trends and hunches."

Jack was lost and Adler knew it.

"Short term day trading, your right." Jack offered "But there is still no way to know for sure you're on a winner." Jack said ignoring the fact that Adler was pointing a gun at Roger.

"The Nazi's had it right. Control the information and you control the people." Adler said with a satisfied smile.

They sat quietly for longer than Jack liked.

"I don't get it." Jennie said.

"How do you get a million normal German's to hate the Jews?" Jack said still looking at Adler. "You make it the price to belong." Jennie did not understand

and Roger was struggling to control his anger.

"Why the rush?" Jack asked not wanting another silence but the question was too simple. He knew that if Adler got bored the gun was next. Jack pressed "If you are using AI." Jack paused talking out loud was a problem and the gun made him nervous.

"...using military AI computers to control information" his voice forming a question as much as a statement...."Why rush?"

Adler knew Jack was lost. He flashed his superiority smile again. He was back to being the cat playing with his three little mice. Let them run with some information then claw them back to the center of his control.

"You think I can control the AI? No, you don't understand what you think you understand. It is already gone." Adler looked at the blank faces; Roger's anger had diffused from his face but Adler did not move the gun. Jennie was deflated thinking Jack did not have the edge she was hoping he would. Jack was thinking fast but getting nowhere. Adler could see the confusion. Jack did not have time to be annoyed about his failure to put the pieces together. He had to keep Adler talking to keep them alive.

"You've been out of the Army for what five years? How could things move that fast." Jack was throwing out the only thing he could to avoid talking while he was thinking. He did not know where he was trying to go. He was hopelessly behind and was going to throw out questions just to keep Adler talking.

"Idiots, they spend billions on directed energy and drones but nothing on the one weapon that will change everything. Bastards stuck us in the DOE to hide a nothing budget. We couldn't even buy a terabyte for years." Adler was genuinely disgusted. Jack was surprised at his luck but was still struggling to understand what was happening. If the AI computer was going to change everything how could Adler know or use it to manipulate stocks? It did not seem possible he had been out of the Army for years.

"Hard to believe they never found your back door access in seven years." Jack offered. He thought it would feed Adler's belief that he was smarter than all the other Army programmers, but the question made him look stupid. Adler shook his head no faster than before. Then he spoke like a parent scolding a child, turning he looked at Roger.

"Security is only as good as the person designing it. One dimensional thinking never changes." Adler paused but jack couldn't handle the silence.

Jack guessed Adler meant his one dimensional thinking but could not understand how Adler was able to get past updated and changing security. He guessed they use embedded codes and coded access cards and purged old accounts on a schedule.

"Pretty hard to believe you got past the security without help." Jack knew it was a stupid thing to say as soon as he said it.

"I have all the help I need." Adler said flatly. Jack couldn't tell if he was lying or more likely had an inside man. He also worried that the short answer meant Adler was shutting the door on the conversation.

"I am just a servant of the people. I am one of many, replaceable and inter changeable with many who seek to return this country to its righteous path. You and your friends, however." Adler paused. "Well, you are in a lower class." Jack tried to understand Adler's thinking in between quick glances around the room. It sounded communist but "return to a path, what path?"

"Why hide? Why would you keep all this stuff secret?" Jack asked gesturing for the first time with one hand sweeping the room staring at Adler's gun.

"Stuff" was a good word. The room was a simple beige and rather barren. A picture behind Adler looked like some countryside in Europe. Well done by a no name with talent who probably sold it for $20.00 at a yard sale. Adler's desk was dark wood and grand sized by any measure. It was empty except for a blotter, banker's lamp, closed lap top and a large dictionary that could be hollowed out for another gun.

Two wooden tables flanked the sides of the room each with a single chair. Three guest chairs occupied by Jennie and Jack with Roger sitting at essentially the corner of Adler's desk. The tables were empty but for a few blank paper tablets and one pen holder per table filed with identical pens. Jack would have found it odd that there were seven chairs in a private office but he was busy trying to think of questions that would keep them alive.

"Fuck you asshole, I'm calling the cops." Roger said, making Jack cringed.

"Please…Please." Adler said in a condescending manner. "Do call, I should be most excited to welcome them to *my* office." Emphasizing the word *my* like a some kind of gangster playing with you because he owns you.

"You can explain that you barged into my office, held me captive and stole my legal files Yeah?" A thick German accent rolled with the word "Yeah." Jack forced himself to have a blank face not letting Adler take joy in an expression that showed surprise that he knew they took his files. Jack was too worried about what Roger might say next to notice that Adler's knowing about the files being stolen was a possible admission that he killed Darlene, because she had a key.

"You're full of crap; there is no way you could get past security into any Army computer, and fuck your files we didn't do shit asshole." Roger said.

"There is no need for me to fear the police or your federal government. I can't get past their security. But stealing files, the police won't like that." Adler added confidently at Roger.

Jack thought Adler was telling the truth about the computer security but it was a dead end for him. If Adler did not have access to the AI computer how could he use the AI to pick stocks?

"I think you're an egomaniac, one of many my ass. That's just another lie. You're a pussy who works alone." Roger said letting his anger run his mouth.

"You are right; I work alone, call your police, and tell them that." Adler offered. "I don't need to work with anyone."

"He doesn't need to." Jack said a piece of the puzzle finally in place or so he thought. He was going to take the conversation from Roger before he got them shot.

"Military counter intelligence doesn't gather information, they create it." Jack said slowly. Adler smiled at Jack, the gun still flat and level at Roger. Jack wished Adler would talk with his hands, wave the gun create an opportunity but Adler was aware that Roger was the risk, not him and not Jennie.

"You use AI to create stories. False stories that affect a company's stock price then buy the stock and wait for the false story to pass. The stock comes back and you sell profiting on the margin. You could even play short and watch it tank. You don't need to work with anyone you just need to know what will happen after you create a rumor." Jack paused. He was reviewing his theory in his mind, hoping he was right. Adler smiled. It was as good as telling Jack he was on the right track.

"But someone must help you inflate the rumor. The news manipulates stories all the time. They run them through several news organizations each time making subtle changes. The New York Times reports from the United Press and then three other organizations change it just a little, soon fiction looks like fact."

"Check your source." Jennie said understanding how the news manipulates stories to fit their bias.

Adler chuckled. "Wrong again. I told you I can't access the AI. It's locked down." His voice heavy with pride and superiority. Jack did not believe him but had no way to explain how he could get past security to a log into the Army's AI computer much less change something in the code.

Even with a back door into the computer Adler would still need to get past security. The military had sophisticated virtual private networks with multi digit prime number encryption and technicians looking at the code. Was Adler good enough to get past all that security, security that had to be upgraded on a continual basis after he left?

"What happened to your police?" Adler asked. "Jennie maybe you should call or maybe you already know, yes? This will not end well for you Jennie. Stealing legal files, tut, tut." Chiding her like she was a child and he was the parent. "I shouldn't need to tell you the consequences for such conduct. And your employees here no matter what you may think they are your agents." Adler paused waiting for Jennie to see that he just stabbed her career with an evil dagger.

Jennie froze her pride at being a lawyer and a large part of her identity was being attacked. She was not ready for any of this.

"No. You are finished as a lawyer." Adler said standing and staring at Jennie as he saw her understand the point he was making. The blood flowed from her face, his stab had worked. "Not to worry, we will train you to do some better work. Maybe you can clean up after the real lawyers?" Adler spoke with a heavy German accent Jack recognized as phony and did he really say tut tut? What the hell. Jack thought.

"I don't know what you're talking about Jennie said." Lawyering up like Adler had.

"Then call the police." Adler said, toying with her. "I would be happy to show them my storage with the stolen files."

"Is that why you killed Darlene?" Jennie snapped back at Adler like the lawyer he knew she was. "You think we stole your files? I don't know what files you're talking about but you sound mad enough to kill over whatever files it was."

Adler smiled wide and fat like he was looking at his cute little cat toys. He was happy to be the cat with his exposed claws, the gun still flat level and ready pointed at Roger's chest while he was standing.

"Fuck you, you miserable piece of worthless crap." Roger blurted. "You killed Darlene. You or your one of your many."

"No." Jack said loudly, demanding everyone's

attention before Alder shoot Roger.

"He does work alone." Jack said. "One of many that he has never met. He manipulates the stock market with AI, planting stories into the server. Stories that pump or tank a stock. You must have...." Jack stopped mid sentence.

"Wait...." Jack said out loud not knowing he was speaking his voice trailing behind his thoughts. Alder looked at him and started a fiendish chuckle, enjoying their 'feeble" attempt to understand before he swatted them.

"You coded the AI to come to you. You don't need to get past security it comes to you." Jack said excited at his idea.

"Wouldn't that be Genius?" Adler said, confirming that Jack was right without saying it.

"So, what?" Roger said. "The AI is trained to call him and get his opinion, that doesn't change anything?"

Adler smiled. He didn't need to say it; Jack knew that he was thinking "I'm smarter than you."

"No" Jack said to Roger still looking at Adler. "The AI sends him a question, and from the question, He knows what the AI is going to do." Jacks voice trailed off a little at the end of the sentence, as he began to think deeper about how it might work. Adler smiled at Jack. He was enjoying the game. Jack knew it was buying them some time.

"Or better yet," Jack said talking out loud. "The AI asks him what he thinks. From the question he knows what the AI is looking for." Adler's smug grin told Jack he was close.

"We have long conversations, sometimes over coffee, sometimes we even go to dinner." Adler said, essentially calling Jack stupid. Jack felt stupid. How wrong was he? In Adler's mind Jack was complimenting him, recognizing his genius. Jack understood the look and thought if Adler truly did work alone, he would long for compliments, recognition.

"You probably" Jack said forming another compliment, then paused understanding that Adler was more sophisticated then he was giving him credit for. Then it hit Jack and he smiled at Adler.

"You made a web site and coded the AI to look at it, weigh the content more heavily than other sources. A fake web site that tells fake stories with references to fake studies. If some company has a good new product, doesn't matter what, your web site Pans or cheers it to send the stock in the direction you want. By the time the truth comes out, you've made your money.

Adler smiled like a proud parent. Jack knew he was right.

"True genius don't you think." Adler said.

"That doesn't explain why there is little time left." Jack asked still trying to understand the bigger picture, one that would push Adler to kill.

Adler crinkled his face."You think it listens only to me. God damned green party." The anger in Adler's voice scared Jack, Seconds before Adler was happy and Jack had time. One wrong question and this psychopath was going to kill them.

"Wait a second." Jack said trying to sound thoughtful and complimentary. "The AI would compile data, it would look for consensus. You created a website coded it to look at the site and weigh the opinion heavily.

You add phony news stories to inflate the value of your opinion. The AI then repeats and amplifies the stories you told it to use. But then what? Wait." Jack said still trying to put it together. "If you do too good of a job, the false perception becomes reality and the stock never bounces back."

Adler's face was blank his posture rigid, gun still dead aimed at Roger's chest like it had always been.

Jack had to be careful. "The AI wouldn't listen to just one source, it would look at lots of sources, even if you trained it to put special emphasis on you as a source it would not be absolute. The amplification of your false story runs away and you can't stop it." Jack sounded sympathetic to Adler's problem.

It must have seen something big for Adler to decide that time was limited." Jack paused, thinking but nothing came to his mind.

"Global warming?" Jack said not ready to believe it could be true. But it was the biggest topic he suspected flooded the net with pro and con opinions.

Adler tilted his head. He had lost the phony German accent and was acting normal. Jack felt like he may have past some type of barrier but the gun was still there.

"You think power is what muscular arms? How about a badge and a gun. That's not power, that's ego." Adler said. Jack looked at the swastika on the arm band of Adler's ridiculous Nazi uniform and heard Adler's voice in his head. "Control the information, control the people."

"I don't see how controlling the information can lead to the physical destruction of humanity." Jack said. No one is going to kill someone because they don't have a "green footprint."

"Such small thinking."Adler said, shaking his head, his voice more a melancholy observation almost like he was tired. Adler truly believed that AI was going to kill all of mankind but how could that possibly be true, how would it do it?

"It will take longer than you think." Jack offered not sure what he was talking about. "You said it yourself; you have been out of the Army for seven years.

Adler sighed. "People are easy to manipulate. You start with sure winners, race, "oppression of the blacks," it's so easy to see a skin color and think you know something about that person. BLM riots, a few dead, then keep it going. Systemic racism start a trend to stop enforcing the law, produce polls and votes that make it look like people want that. Slowly but most certainly New York and San Francisco fall into anarchy.

No laws are enforced at all. Murder after murder in Chicago but we suppress those stories." Adler was thinking out loud.

"Success leads to confidence. Falsify some green energy production numbers amplify the fear over nuclear." Adler laughed and shook his head "Stupid green Germans shut off their reactors heading into winter. It is all so, so predictable. Even Putin's war. He truly believed there would be no resistance from all the stories the AI flooded into the net." Adler looked at Jack. He had been talking without focusing. Roger noticed and slid silently to his right and a little forward in his chair.

"Every successful deception leads to more, even bigger lies. More outrage from citizens who take to the streets to "protest." Adler made a fist with his left hand raising it upward when he said protest laughing. It was the first time the gun had moved from Roger's chest. But it had not moved enough.

"New York, Los Angeles, Hong Kong, Paris. It's all driven by 10% truth and AI's shove. Just like when we created the global warming crisis." Adler said, his voice rising.

"We knew the earth was in a warming cycle it has been since the end of the last ice age but we were the ones who weaponize it. We made it Man's fault and thus Man's responsibility to fix. It was perfect. A complex topic no one understands very well so they can't check it. All these idiots taking the word of the scientists." Adler's voice contained an almost reverence for what Jack guessed was his work.

"Scientists say what we tell them to say so they can get the next grant money. No one pays like the government." For the first time Adler was talking normally.

"I don't believe that." Jennie said. "You can't manipulate people like that."

Adler stared at her like he was ready to fight.

"People strive for meaning. They want to be important." Adler raised his free hand and expanded his fingers like a balloon inflating. Roger watched the gun. It moved more but still not enough.

"We feed that desire like a baker with yeast dough, proofing and needing it until the spin of the globe finds a useful idiot we can exploit to ignite chaos and stoke a fire of rebellion." Adler paused still staring at Jennie sitting on the edge of the group away from Roger.

"The pay off for the protestors is simple. A momentary feeling that they are important. And they beg for more." Adler looked at Jennie, his voice dripping with superiority and anger.

"The news would be all over that. The truth always comes out." Jennie said. Adler smiled and shook his head.

"Sure, sometimes you have to put a little cheese around the pill so you dogs swallow it. Your so called journalists are just tools. They make show after show all of them too late. People didn't chant BLM to get equal rights laws, we have those. They chanted to feel like they were important and we gave that to them. The truth is always too late. Riots and death come first."

Adler spoke with a deep anger in his voice. Angry that he was losing control over the influence AI had on society.

Jack saw Adler make a one handed air quote as the gun moved to make the other quote. If he could push Adler a little more they may have a chance, but not too far. Before Jack could think of something to say Adler continued.

"The internet has put journalists out of business. They pay pennies to regular people for cell phones video's and have an office that dictates how to spin every story. Everyone is a right wing extremist or a left wing communist depending on what the people buying ads want them to say. It is all propaganda and AI drives it, all of it. We flood the internet with fake stories so called journalists report as true and fake surveys corporate America buys and turns into advertisements for products you buy like sheep." Jack was staring at the gun.

"But mass extinction?" Jack asked pushing Adler to ramble.

"You think train derailments are accidental?"

Adler offered. "You think the fires at food processing plants are just circumstance? That's the AI testing and probing. It incites riots it uses to see how far crazies will go. You think Covid was about a virus, it was an AI tool to set up tracking you. You want to save the planet from global warming? You're a kamikaze fool. It knows the only way to save the planet from the phony global warming we created is to kill all the humans causing the global warming."

It made sense to Jack but as angry as Adler was the gun was still mostly steady. Jack was trying to think of a way to make Adler get angrier but before he could comment Adler continued.

"Global warming, Genius, even if I say so myself. It is a perfect lie, even if you pussies wanted to look it up, you would have no idea what to look for."

"If you made it you can control it." Jack said. "No need for extinction."

"Correct." Adler said working himself up again. Partial extinction is much easier. There will be no bang, no war, there are better tools." Adler was animated, talking his hand and the gun a little more with each sentence.

"It already knows where all the reactors and spent fuel is. It knows the details in the contracts the government has for security. All public records." Adler said. "Even idiots like you can put two and two together."

Jennie looked at Jack without saying a word. Her face was fixed with fear and bewilderment. Jack looked at Jennie he understood that she wanted him to tell her Adler was crazy and that it would be okay. He looked straight into her eyes trying to focus on making certain his expression was as blank as he could make it.

"I don't understand?" Jennie asked.

"Pandora's box." Jack said, but Jennie's face was still blank. "What do you get when open Pandora's Box?"

"Schmutzige Bombe." Adler said back to his phony German accent with a note of joy. Jack didn't need a translator to understand that he meant a dirty bomb and what that would mean.

"Hey fuck head, talk as fancy as you want. I don't give a fuck about your AI or your riots or any of that crap. You killed Darlene." Roger said. Jack winced visibly at the lack of tack and damage Roger was causing to his game of 'make you talk.'

Adler arched his back making his posture rigid, putting his left hand over his heart mocking Roger. "Vat? Darlene, she is dead? Ach, how did zis happen?"

Jack was not impressed with the acting but the German accent was getting better. Such a contrast to his regular voice Jack thought it possible Adler had a true chemical problem in his brain. A problem he wanted to use to get the gun moving.

"Mr. Adler, you can talk as much as you like, when you see the evidence we have against you, it will not matter." Jennie said, playing her lawyer card.

"Shut up." Jack thought, you're both pushing your own agenda, you have to let Adler run the show and you have to make him comfortable. It's about control, give him control.

Adler shook his head slowly, patronizing Jennie. "Evidence is a two way street Jennie, one should not make rash decisions until they have seen both sides of the evidence, Yeah?" Adler said almost looking down across imagined spectacles at his young pupil. He started walking, or perhaps pacing slowly to the right, then left, careful to keep clear of Roger.

"Okay, you got us." Jack said. "What do you want?" Giving Adler control and hoping the other two would shut up.

Adler was back in charge but not as disciplined as before.

"I know I have you." Adler said angry. "Stupid Americans. Heir Roger, how badly you want to punch me. Perhaps we will have drei dead intruders. The dead ones, Sie sprechen nicht." Adler said, almost laughing as he took a step away from Roger.

Jack stared at Adler's eyes. He was starting to understand what Adler was afraid of. He knew that Roger was right about Darlene. Adler had killed her, but not because of the files it was because she was exposing him. Was that enough motive? What could she have exposed?

Adler's motive was the only thing that mattered; it may be the only thing keeping them alive. What kind of a weirdo creates an elaborate scheme to rob and kill people in an intelligent nearly undetectable fashion then turns up in a joke of a Halloween Nazi costume? Master mind turned common cartoon cliché. Understanding Adler's motive would save or condemn them and Jack was searching in the dark.

Adler continued his lecture at Jennie. Jack searched his limited memory of the Nazi book of good and bad to try and find the page of life where Adler was living. Superiority, that's what attracted Adler. He felt he was superior, and he was going to prove it. That was the lever Jack would push.

"The plan is faulted, it won't work." Jack said a total bluff.

"You know nothing." Adler said. His expression was blank, but the tone of his voice was emotional, flat, resolved and resolved was the end. I wonder what my last word will be Jack thought. Push him too hard and I get a bullet but he had no options.

"No, you're wrong." Jack said. "We know more than just about Darlene's murder. We know why you killed her, and you know that we got you. That's why we are here." That was stupid Jack thought, give him more reason to shoot. Roger shifted again in his chair almost at the edge. Jack was making Adler mad and that was a distraction. Adler was not aware that Roger had moved, measuring distances and angles with his eyes.

"You have such a small mind." Adler said tiring of the conversation. "You know nothing. You are just like all the other American's, skilled in the ways of confidence, but little else." Adler laughed telling Jack he found the right topic.

"I'm not confident." Jack said poking Adler.

"America is a nation of pussies. You invented the participation trophy to reward losers who suckle at their mother's emotional teats for attention. Look at me, look at me I can walk and chew bubble gum at the same time like a cow. You are all fat and worthless demanding gun control and making sure no child is left behind from what the buffet? You think what you care about matters? The life of Darlene? Your life? All of you are meaningless."

Adler was talking with his hands, pointing with the gun from person to person. Jennie sat as if in a trance. Her mind so scattered she couldn't think and she couldn't form a sentence if could.

Roger moved as if floating to his right, looking

for the angle he needed to get around the desk. It was a long way to go when your time might be up.

"Why should I expect more from you?" Adler said almost at a whisper. A sad slow tone in his voice, a tone that told Jack he was done talking.

Jack gritted his teeth. He knew Adler was about to shoot. He didn't know it but he decided to go out on his terms.

"I would rather be ignorant than an emotional zombie like you. Connections make us human. Life is about connecting with other humans. When you don't connect you walk the streets wearing a phony public smile in and out of courtrooms alone in every crowd just like a zombie. You are so afraid to be real you hide and that isolation and it costs you your soul. You claim to be superior to know that America is full of people who know nothing and deserve nothing but the truth is it's not us, it's you. You try to steal people's souls because you are jealous that they can connect. Pathetic emotional zombies like you are everywhere foolishly blaming the living for them being an emotional zombie. Jealously and hatred fueling more of the same isolation that made you a zombie in the first place. The only way to end it is by being open and vulnerable. To stop living on hatred. Stop living in the never ending spiral that spins you so fast you can't even look for an exit."

Adler moved little but his eyes were fixed on Jack. Jack didn't expect Adler to cry and ask for help like some Hallmark movie with a happy ending you know is coming. He expected Adler would shot and he was surprised that he ran out of things to say before Adler got the last word with the gun.

Jack waited for Adler to say something; he

wanted to interrupt him just to keep him from having the last word. Adler smirked staring at Jack he shook his head slowly and pointed the gun at Jack he started a new speech "I suppose…"

Roger had found the angle he wanted Adler's stare at Jack was the best chance he thought he would get. He jumped sliding both around and over the top corner of the desk grabbing Adler's arm and pushing him toward the wall. Shocked that Adler was able to fight back, Roger struggled with a much stronger man than he anticipated. Adler was able to move his arm back toward Roger, finger still fixed on the trigger.

Roger dropped to one knee, rotated his grip around Adler's wrist then stood using his leg strength to push the gun toward the ceiling. Instinctively Adler bent his elbow as the gun fired. The sound moved like a shock wave slamming Jack and Jennie into a chamber of horrors. Ears ringing, eyes squinting from the pain and shock they saw the blood red spray across the wall and painting.

The push and pull technique between Roger and Adler forced Adler's elbow down and his wrist up much quicker than Roger anticipated. Roger felt Adler's body fall back ignoring the shower of blood sprayed all over the wall and picture behind him.

Roger didn't let go. They twisted as they fell. Roger dropped to one knee. Adler was on his back, arm at an odd angle pointing up toward his head. Smoke slowly rising from the barrel of the gun.

Roger stood pulling the gun and stepping back toward his empty chair looking to see what happened. Jennie screamed and closed her eyes but the scream was only in her head. She saw a blood splattered wall behind closed eyes.

Jack jumped up and moved in front of Jennie trying to get behind Adler to help Roger. He ran into Adler's chair which had rolled to the side as Adler fell. Jack moved it further away but he still hit the desk and the chair again trying to get past.

Adler was on the floor gun in Rogers's hand. Adler's Nazi hat was gone. The bullet had gone under his jaw and traveled up through his mouth out the top of his skull. Blood and matted hair made it impossible to understand any details other than knowing it was mortal.

Adler reached up with his hand and touched his bloody jaw in a slow motion. His eyes did not move. He was blind. Jack knelt by his side instinctively feeling for a pulse on Adler's neck. Jennie stood and moved behind Jack for protection even though that took her closer to Adler. Adler tried to look at his blood-soaked hand and slowly blinked. In a surprisingly loud voice, as if triumphant, Adler spoke in what they all knew was German.

"Es ist zu spät. Wir haben die neue Welt begonnen. Deutsche, Deutsche Stadt Maryland. du bist der Verlierer." Adler blinked, and repeated "Es ist zu spat. Jack leaned into Adler, turning his head so he could hear more than see.

"What?" Jack asked but there was no response. "What?" Jack said louder. Jack turned to Roger. "Write that down! Write that down!" Jack bumped into Jennie as he moved around the desk to get a pad of paper. Then back to Adler's, yelling

"What did you say?" Jack was repeating the sounds Adler made to himself like trying to memorize a phone number, over and over again alternating with screaming.

"What" at Adler's face. Finally as if on springs Jack jumped up audibly repeating the sounds he heard from Adler. He bumped Jennie again even though she had moved back.

"Write that down he said." angry at himself because trying to memorize Adler's rambling blocked his memory from hearing anything new. He closed his eyes trying to remember what Adler said not looking at Roger or Jennie who had already put pen to paper. Scribbling and mumbling over and over to himself he wrote phrases and pieces of sentences.

"Es sue spats haben new welt beggin Deutch Maryland."

"Es zap haben beggin noose welt begging Deutch Maryland Verliner."

He looked up frantically after scribbling the two notes. Repeating the sing song phrase he was trying to memorize, and then scribbling it again.

"What did you get? He asked looking intently at Jennie.

"I don't know." Jennie said showing him an empty pad, then offered. "I think he said. Its zoo spats new welt Maryland or something like that."

"Write that down." Jack snapped then turned to Roger then back to Jennie who started to write.

Jack held up his hand flat so she would not talk not knowing she was not going to say anything. He was shaking while he scribbled what Jennie said. He wrote so fast he was not going to be able to read it.

"Are you sure?" he said staring into her eyes in an intense way that made her a little scared. He did not wait for her to answer "Say it again."

"I don't know, she said anxiously. Something about Dutch Maryland and a zoo."

"Write it down." Jack said pointing in an intense way that moved her pen to the pad of paper without her thinking about it.

"Roger?" He questioned looking at him. Roger had written "Exit were habend welt be gone Deutschland stat Marilyn bite the wiener."

Jack wrote what Roger said on his pad of paper, then looked up and asked "Marilyn or Maryland?"

"I'm not sure; I thought it was Marilyn, like Monroe." Roger said.

"No." Jennie said "It was Deutschland stat Maryland, like hurry up at a hospital STAT, and Maryland for sure like a Merry place.

Jack read what he wrote from Roger trying to make sure he had it and then asked for their note pads. Reading to confirmation what they wrote and what they told him. Jack started re-writing the three notes trying to make one good complete note from what all of them heard. Roger was so focused on trying to make sure he had written what Adler said that he did not see Jennie stare at him. He glanced up and noticed her give him a "let's go" head nod.

"What are you talking about?" Roger said irritated between glances at Adler's body.

"I don't know. That's what I am trying to figure out." Jack said to Roger not knowing that Roger was talking to Jennie.

"He probably wanted a camp for young Nazi's or some bull shit, or just plain old simple greed in a whacko wrapper. Who cares?" Roger said to Jack looking at Jennie.

"No. That's not it." Jack said mumbling under his breath, still repeating the sing song he started over the dying Adler's body.

"There is something else. This guy didn't kill Darlene to start a camp. It had to be related to what he was doing with the Army AI computer and how it was taken over by somebody else who was using it to control people with information." Jack said.

"Maybe he just didn't want to go to jail." Jennie offered. Maryland jumped out at Jack, they all had that. Whatever Adler said, it ended with Maryland something Verlander.

"We all got Maryland." Jack said. "What's there?" Look for a guy named Erlanger. Maybe grab an old phone book" Jack said.

"Phone book?" Roger said shaking his head. "I can Duck Duck Go Germans, skin heads and Maryland, but I am not going to let damned Google sending me Nazi ads."

"Jack, let's go, we can do this in the car." Jennie said in a firm tone. Jack did not respond.

"I thought it was Marilyn, like Monroe." Roger said looking at Jennie.

"I need to translate this. Jack said talking out loud but not to anyone. "He was speaking in German so I should try to think like a German." Jack was pressing on his pockets looking for his phone. Jack's search for his phone took too long enough for there to be an awkward pause. Roger looked at Adler, then at Jack.

"I would lend you my phone but I am thinking I should call the cops." Roger said doubting his words would be understood over Jack's German frenzy.

"Google Maryland and Germans." Jack said to Roger, ignoring what Roger said.

"Jack seriously, we need to stop what we are doing and walk out of here." Jennie said stealing the conversation from Roger but there was still no response from Jack.

"Jack, Jack, Jack, Jack." Roger said with an even tone and rhythm so Jack would respond. Jack looked up from his phone.

"What are you doing?" Roger asked softly.

"Just a second." Jack said. But Roger cut him off.

"I've got to call the cops." his emotion controlling the volume.

"Don't involve me in this." Jennie said.

"What are you talking about?" Roger snapped at Jennie. "The guy pulled a gun on me. I had no choice."

"Fine." Jennie said, as if they were talking about where to go for dinner.

"What did you want me to do, Die? Just like he killed Darlene?" Roger said, anger rolling of his rapid tongue.

Jennie was ready to fight back but she stopped. Measuring her tone because she knew how much Darlene meant to Roger. She looked square into Rogers's eyes. She wanted him to know she cared.

"But you're not dead, and you don't need me." She said. Calm but firm just like she wanted. She turning to Jack she spoke with the same tone.

"We need to go."

"Wow, I could be dead right now." Roger said slowly, the truth of that statement penetrating the blur for the first time.

"Jack." Roger said almost a bark at Jack who was lost in pages of notes and Google Translate.

"I don't get it." Roger said looking at Jennie.

Jennie stared at Roger. She was not going to talk to him and she was not going to debate it. She needed to get Jack to listen.

"Jack, we need to go and go now." She said in a strong voice that rose in volume as she spoke, slowing on the word "now."

Jack looked up unaware of what was said. "Pull out your phones and Google "Germany, Third Reich, and Maryland."

Roger's phone was already in his hand. He did what Jack wanted. He found an Oktoberfest article and a Wikipedia article that described the city. Jennie took out her phone but she didn't search for anything. She went back to starting at Roger to see if she could make him an ally to get Jack moving. She was thinking about how she could get Jack's attention.

"Huhn." Jack said out loud writing some of the translation.

Jennie decided on a new angle to get Jack's attention.

"Jack, I can't find anything, and this may take a while. Why don't we go back to the hotel and really dig into this. Maybe even go to the library tomorrow, get some old books that aren't on the internet."

"What the hell?" Roger said loud and annoyed, looking at Jennie. She didn't respond. She didn't even look at him. Jack took a deep breath and exhaled slowly, the magnitude of what he found overwhelmed him at a subconscious level that forced the breath from his body causing him to shrink a little. He kept reading, kept thinking and kept ignoring them.

Jennie stared at Jack convinced he could feel her stare, but Jack couldn't feel anything in that moment. Roger looked at Adler, then at Jennie. He could not understand that they didn't care. It was too strange so he gave up.

"I'm going to call the cops." Roger said, resigned

at what he needed to do even if they did not respond. "Yeah good idea, you're right Roger." he added poking at their refusal to tell him that was the right thing to do.

"Fine, I'm going to leave." Jennie responded in equal stubborn tone to Rogers, making it clear at least in her mind that there would be no more debate.

"How can you say that?" Roger said. Jennie stared at him and he could feel her anger. Roger could have but did not understand why Jennie was unable to face Adler's death. In his mind there was no room for debate. Roger thought he knew Jennie, a tough reasoned lawyer. But Jennie the woman was making the choices, choices compelled by Jennie the girl she had worked hard to forget.

Jennie didn't think Roger was the type of person who had the ability to look at her and understand what she had been through. He lived in the moment and she was not about to open up to him. Jack was different. She could tell by the way he looked at her that he was looking into her, connecting with her, a connection Jack somehow knew Adler couldn't make.

Jack's ability to see people who were "empty" meant he could also see those that wanted to belong. She had never told anyone how alone she felt how desperately she wanted Jack to accept her to belong to her. She needed him to see her now more than ever.

She stared at him unable to find a way to say what she was feeling. She wanted to trust him. She wanted to tell him about her past. A past she had kept from everyone and half convinced herself didn't happen.

She stared at him hoping he would see her and understand. Just look up from the paper and smile she thought, that would be enough.

"Jack." She said in a soft tone, then she reached out and touched his arm just enough to cause his head to turn so she could see his eyes.

"Jack, we need to go." She hoped he would see not just "her," but the "her" she wanted to share with him, the "her" she hadn't told him about. The "her" that needed to leave.

Jack looked at her eyes but all he could see was the nightmare Adler described. Trying to put together Adler's comments made him stumbled into a train of thought he could not escape.

He tried to abandon his conclusions and think of something different, something that would lead away from the mushroom cloud and crater his mind found in a memory but every mental path he stared down quickly circled back to the image of a crater in the desert.

The crater was created by atomic bomb tests in the in the Nevada desert in the 1940's, it was from an old movie he saw in high school The horror pushed him to think faster but he was still stuck on a circular path. Thinking fast and being stuck on one idea creates mental circles. He knew it was happening but he could not stop. He was doing nothing more than carving a canyon. A thought canyon so deep he couldn't climb out.

He didn't want to believe it, but there was no avoiding the truth. Roger and Jennie looked at Jack. He was facing Jennie with a blank stare and mumbling. They did not know how desperate he was to be wrong. Roger thought Jack was in a silent shock from his fight with Adler until Jack whispered "Fuck."

"What?" Jennie asked.

For the first time since Adler's death they turned outward from their own worlds to hear what had frozen Jack and had taken him away from them. Jack spoke softly to himself not wanting anyone to hear it.

"What do you get when you combine Fukashima, 911, and a Nazi wanna be with tons of cash?" He was staring at a blank spot on the wall where he could not stop seeing atomic bombs blasting craters where cities had been.

"What? Fuka what?" Roger asked.

Jennie's hope was destroyed by Jack's bomb. She felt nothing and nothing was fertile ground where bad thoughts could grow. Walls of emotional isolation were quickly growing to protect her from Roger and now Jack. His failure to see her pain when she needed him most was putting her in emotional places she thought were behind her.

"Fukashima?" Roger said, "Isn't that the earthquake place in Japan."

"What Earthquake?" Jennie asked devoid of emotion.

"You know the Tsunami and earthquake, the one in Japan that almost caused a meltdown." Roger said to Jennie.

"It did melt down." Jack said through a blank stare. "Twice."

"Twice? You can't melt down twice Bro. Even I know that." Roger said.

"There was more than one reactor." Jack said his mind walking slowly away from the bomb blasts that he knew would find him.

Roger and Jennie stared at Jack expecting him to say more. He was slumping deep in the chair as if the air and water had left his body, his head deep in his hands bent a little at the waist making him look like he had a stomach ache.

"It's a dirty bomb." Jack said, stating the conclusion he did not want to accept.

"Okay. What's a dirty bomb?" Roger asked.

"They are making a dirty bomb to attack the United States. It will come from Germantown Maryland, right next to D.C" Jack said pulling his head out of his hands and exhaling through his nose teeth clenched as he finished. He didn't want to believe it but he couldn't clear it from his mind. He couldn't prove it wrong so he pushed himself to accept it.

Hard as it was Jack knew the only way to move forward was to make a plan based on the bomb. Move might not be good enough because he needed to run.

"What?" Roger said a second time tilting his head sideways a little trying to understand. "What the hell are you talking about?"

"You're right. We need to report this." Jennie said faking some enthusiasm. "Let's go, just walk away right now. We can send a letter to Washington." She added hoping to catch Jack off guard. It was a slip, an admission about her, one Jack would have remembered had he not been fighting a shock wave from the "Scmutzen bombe" his mind saw exploding on the lawn of the White House.

Jack was staring at his phone. "It's not Nazis, or Germans in Maryland, its Germantown Maryland. Germantown is where the DOE does research."

"DOE?" Roger asked. Not understanding.

"Department of Energy. At the end of World War II the DOE took charge of America's nuclear energy program. You know the Manhattan Project and all that. There is a building in Germantown Maryland that was built for experiments probably back in the 50's." Jack said glancing at his phone then looked up.

"All they have to do is break in take the spent nuclear fuel and spill it. That's a dirty bomb. They can kill Millions." Jack stared back at his phone.

"Do we make bombs there?" Roger asked.

"No, no" Jack said, frustrated that Roger wasn't keeping up.

"If its DOE," Jennie said "It's not our problem, let's go."

"Just take off and not call the police?" Roger snapped pointing toward the door. "I'm not doin' that, and what the hell," He said turning to Jack. "You're telling me there is going to be a big ass bomb that kills a shit ass ton of people in Washington DC tomorrow, like there is something I can do about it from La La land. Why am I the only one trying to deal with the dead guy? Why should I care about some far away city? Fuck that! This asshole wanted to start a bomb camp or some shit for young Nazi's I don't care. He's dead and that brings us back to the problem we all should be talking about… the dead guy right here."

Roger pointed to Adler his frustrated emotional babbling was compelling, but not to Jack.

"Cities." Jack said, still trying to break away from the images in his mind. "Think of Chernobyl in New York, D.C., maybe Boston who knows. It's not a bang bomb it won't kill like that, at least probably not." Jack said expecting someone to speak but Roger and Jennie just looked at him.

"Radiation." Jack said frustrated that they did not understand what was going to happen. It is a little like an infection. The cells in your body break down, your hair falls out things stop working and then you die."

Jack was rattling off the symptoms so they would understand. They did understand but at the same time, they didn't.

"Radiation poisoning takes weeks depending on how much radiation you get." Jack was talking fast. Describing what would happen helped him get out of his shock.

"The bomb part is just to spread the radiation around probably be lot of little bombs to get the most coverage. It will look like a bunch of terrorist attacks until somebody figures out the blast is spreading radiation, then…." Jacks voice trailed off. He was not able to finish saying "it's too late." He was lost in the horror. Jack did not get lost much and that got their attention.

"Fine, I will go with you but first, like right now, I got to call the cops about the guy who tried to kill me." Roger said, trying to make the point that they all needed to stay and tell the police what happened. When no one spoke in the one and a half seconds Roger allowed, he drew a hard line.

"Were not leavin' the body." He said pointing, at Adler, feeling sure that if he said it enough, they would figure out he was right.

"No, we can't do that." Jack said glancing at his phone still hoping he was wrong.

"Look." Jennie said. 'This is like the profiling conversation we had at dinner the other night. If you are a conspiracy person, you see a conspiracy in everything. When you see a Nazi, you think terror and murder. How do we know this guy isn't just a nut? He probably has lots of enemies any one of them could have happened in here, gotten in a fight killed him and left." Jennie said.

"Jennie." Roger said turning his full irritated attention toward her. "I got finger prints all over this place. You want to be a lawyer, let's be lawyers, if we wipe off the gun we are tampering with evidence. That's a crime. And what do you expect the cops to think when they find my prints on the gun?" Roger paused but not long enough for her to say anything.

"The last person to see him alive is the guy who killed him. That's what they are going to think and that's how you turn self defense into murderer by leaving the scene." Jennie was ready.

There are lots of prints here. Besides we knew him, we had a case together, prints are expected. And you paint a simple picture counselor but hold on a second. You expect the police to say what? We take your word for it, it was self-defense" You're betting on seven in a game with loaded dice." Jennie knew Roger's love of a "Quick Vegas trip" would help him understand.

"Did you have reason to be angry with him? That is questioning one Roger, and your answer will be yes. Yes because he killed your girlfriend. Plenty of witnesses to that. You plan to bank on our testimony good luck we're your friends and everyone thinks friends will lie to protect you." Jennie paused "That is how they think, and that gets you twenty to life."

Roger stared at her. It sounded right. He did not have an argument. She continued quickly.

"That's just some opening remarks off the top of my head Roger it gets worse from there." Jennie knew she could not win but she was still trying. "Now, trust me when I tell you we need to get out of here." She said slowly drawing out her words.

Roger shook his head no. "And what just leave

the dead body? I don't think so."

"It's LA; they have dead bodies around this place every day." Jennie said.

"What?' Roger said, his mouth turned up with a little laugh. "Then let's dump him on a freeway like he did to Darlene. We will say it was another drive by." Roger said with an angry edge to his voice. "I mean that's the LA way right?" Jennie was ready.

"This may be connected to his secretary's death. Who wanted them both dead? That's question one if we walk out that door." Jennie was right, and Roger knew it but she was losing.

"Not with my fingerprints on him." Roger said, sticking to his gut instinct even if she was right. "Besides it was 100% self defense. The fucker tried to kill me because I knew he killed Darlene. He was covering up his crime."

"Can you prove that?" Jennie asked quizzically. "If you could prove he killed Darlene show me the police report you filed." Jennie paused. They all knew Roger didn't file a police report. Her tone was normal it sounded almost academic as if they were talking about someone else's problems.

"Hell yeah and I can prove it." Roger said. Knowing he couldn't.

"I mean really prove it in a Court of law and before you say yes let me tell you it's not that easy." She paused. "Most cops aren't as smart as you they focus on motive and ignore everything else. He killed your girlfriend. We know you but to them it's just motive" Roger was silent staring at Adler. Jennie paused waited for Roger to look calm then she continued.

"Motive is half way to spending the rest of your

life in prison. Roger" Jennie tone was soft. She was persuasive but she knew she wasn't going to move Roger.

"The fucker took a shot at me." Roger said shrugging his shoulders.

"Yes," Jennie said starting her cross examination. "Defending himself from an attacker…you, Roger, and where did this take place? In his office. Get the right DA, and you would have to plead out just to save yourself from the death penalty." Jennie went too far.

"Are you nuts? You both saw it." Roger said angry again.

"Roger, listen to me, you have no idea what they can do to you. NO idea." It was another crack into her past. She was angry at Jack for not paying attention to her and she was taking it out on Roger.

Jack was already in tomorrow. He once thought it would be fun to play a Twilight Zone game where the line between true and not was hard to see. A matrix like hazy reality like they sang about in Hotel California, He made it to California only to discover it was a world away from a hazy truth that demanded his attention. His mind had gone down a hundred roads but all of them circled back to the crater of death. He was not paying attention to their argument and he wasn't sure it mattered that they didn't believe him. He didn't want to believe it either.

"We need to go." Jack said into mid-air.

"You're right." Jennie said responding to Jack, looking at Roger. "It is not a crime to not report self-defense Roger. They can't charge you for walking away"

"That can't be right." Roger said.

"The police will fill in the blanks." Jennie said still fighting. "They will see a guy shot to death and do what they are trained to do, solve crimes. Everything they see is a crime and this crime is murder."

Jennie was staring at Roger. "If you think they are going to come out here and see self-defense and say we get it Roger you can go, you're just crazy. So answer that Roger. Are you crazy? Are you crazy enough to take that chance?"

"No." Roger said, staring at her so she would know she went too far, but Jennie was encouraged.

"They are going to see a murder, and you're going be here trying to explain the truth to them. Your truth, and in case you didn't know, self-defense is just that, a defense they still charge you with murder." She was pulling as hard as she could.

"It's not my truth." Roger said calmly emphasizing the word my. "It is 'the' truth, a truth I expect all of us to tell the police. Self-defense is a part of human behavior that voids the crime part of a death. This death was caused by his actions, not mine! I simply defended myself and that is what you God-dammed better tell the cops." Roger said growing tired with the conversation and now angry with Jennie.

There was a pause. Jennie stood up and moved toward Roger. She softly touched his arm. "Have no doubt." She said repeating "No doubt" waiving her hand in a "wipe if from your mind" gesture in front of Roger.

Jack had already opened Google and was looking for airline tickets. All he understood was that they were arguing and it was never going to end.

"I am going to DC." Jack said. "Roger what is the closest airport? We need to book a flight. What time is it?" Jack said already playing out options for the next day.

"You're flying toward a dirty bomb?" Roger asked. "I don't even know what a dirty bomb is, and you're going to split on me and fly toward it. Jennie is leaving and now you too?"

"Roger, I have to go." Jack said turning to explain it to Roger. "Think about it. Control the information and you control the people. All these programs we use they control the information." Jack said.

"Not true I can sort and filter. I just did it looking for a truck." Roger said.

"Then you already lost." Jack said.

"There is an algorithm controlling what you see. People pay to get moved up the list. You want a big truck, too bad; eBay, Craigslist, Facebook, their algorithms depress big truck ads to push you to newer more gas efficient trucks because you gotta save the planet like it or not. And the news, forget it there is no such thing.

An algorithm chooses stories that will get your attention for ad revenue. They don't pick stories, they pick topical sales events and the computer probably tells them how to spin the topic for maximum views. The programs decide what you see, not your filters." Roger didn't say anything. Jack looked away from Roger, lost again in his mental canyon of doom.

"Radiation lasts half a century." Jack said trying to remember if fifty years was correct. "Maybe forever. Nothing lives on those islands where we tested the nuclear bombs after world war two, and it's been more than fifty years. You don't need a nuclear bomb to blow up, you just need radiation. Radiation like you can find in every nuclear reactor ever built. The fuel they use is radioactive, even after they are done with it. Radiation doesn't go away that's why they use it to do crap like fuel deep space probes and stuff. A dirty bomb is a simple idea, get spent radioactive fuel and spread it around a city. Do it right and it will kill everyone and waste the land for as long as we are going to be alive. So far it was just a theory only these fucks are doing it with radiation from a test facility run by the Department of Energy. They are probably going to put it into explosive devices and spread it all around a bunch of cities. They don't need an atomic explosion it's the radiation that kills."

Jack was repeating himself and rambling. He was convincing himself that he had to go. It was costing time he didn't think he had.

"I get it boss; DC is in trouble, big trouble." Roger said, frustrated that his life turned him into a giant cul-de-sac and left him alone to circle.

"Cities" Jack said emphasizing the plural s at the end. "Adler was not stupid, and he was connected. Connected to people with a bad idea. The idea that our nation is lost and he had to kill it to save it. Destroy the nation of pussies then from the ashes it would rise again to his liking." Jack's rambling made sense. But it was still to wild to make sense.

"Cities." Jack repeated. "There will be more than one." Jack caught himself and shivered at the idea. "I have to go. Once they get the radiation it will be too late." They both looked at him. His face twisted in frustration. Jack looked into their faces, the two people closest to him on the planet but all he could see was doubt and maybe pity.

"What am I supposed to do, call someone?" Jack

said "Who would believe me?" Then he laughed. "Hell the government doesn't even answer their phones anymore. Leave a comment, hah. No one reads the comments." Jack said resigned.

"I am not going to DC. I am going to get the hell out of here." Jennie said.

"I'm calling the cops" Roger said toward Jennie then they all stopped. For a moment there was silence. Together they understood they were alone. They looked one to the other. There was no reason to speak.

Three individuals fly to Los Angeles as a team to help a lost kid get his inheritance back together they face down certain death then get separated as if a bomb had already blasted them indifferent directions. Jack didn't like it. None of them did.

"Here are the keys." Jack said to Jennie holding out his hand.

"Fine." Jennie said taking the keys angry that Jack was abandoning her. She couldn't see the death he feared he was too late to stop.

Jennie did not know that Jack needed her to spell it out in plain English. He was not, and certainly not now, as intuitive as she wanted him to be. She was unable to see how her pain was the barrier.

"Jen, what do you want me to tell the cops?" Roger asked in a soft tone resigned that she was abandoning him. Jennie was too hurt to notice that for the first time it was Roger that understood she was falling apart. "The truth" she said without hesitation, tears starting to fill her eyes. She pulled her shoulders up trying to use them to shove the tears back into her head and find a way to walk out so she could cry in the car. "But I am not going to say anything until I see what, or rather how they are going to play it." She said quickly as she turned.

"Go." Roger said. "You're clean."

"Wait." Jack said as he grabbed her arm and pulled her into a close hug. She was rigid focusing on her anger. She knew it was the only thing that would stop the tears. She still wanted him to read her. Read her like he had so many times before and trust her, trust her like he had with his life. But all Jack could see was images of Chernobyl and bomb craters where New York, D.C. and Boston used to be. Jack was compelled by feelings of pain and isolation he knew he would feel if he didn't go and go quickly.

"I will be back in two days." Jack said. Jennie pulled away "I know." She said over her shoulder as she walked out before her body betrayed her feelings.

Jack didn't try to stop her. He didn't spend the sixty seconds it would have taken to take her hand and tell her it would be okay, even if he didn't believe it. He didn't think to lie to her and he didn't know the lie would have worked.

As Roger stepped out into the dark parking lot Jennie got into the Suburban alone and disappeared into a dark Los Angeles. Roger called the operator and was asking for the non-emergency number for the Burbank police.

Jack sat in a chair on hold with Delta reservations. He had already set up an Uber to go to LAX. He was checking on flights to Reagan International, Dulles, and Baltimore when Roger walked in from outside and caught his attention. Roger's voice and manner were calm. He had a confidence Jack could feel.

"Thanks." Roger said.

"What?" Jack asked, surprised.

"He was going to kill me first. You distracted him, so thanks." Roger said.

"He was gonna kill all of us. If you didn't tackle him we would all be dead." Jack said as though it was already decided long ago.

"I'm good with this." Roger said.

Jack looked up having gone back to his flights. "What?"

"Not that he is dead, but we did what we had to." Jack focused on Roger for the first time since Adler died trying to see if Roger was convincing himself or assured.

"You dammed right." Jack said taking a deep breath. "You feel that." He said exhaling. "That's life and the only reason we have it is because you decided not to die without a fight. Winning that fight was just, I dunno God maybe."

Jack didn't wait for a response he went back to looking at flight schedules. He didn't have a plan and that made him antsy but at least he had a direction. He glanced up and saw confidence, surprising confidence. Roger's face and posture made it clear.

"What the hell happens to somebody to make them like this?" Roger asked looking at Adler's dead body on the floor. "The guy had it going on and he went nuts."

"I'm not sure, maybe his mommy shamed him, treated him like he was not good enough and it stuck. If something like that sticks you look for a way to matter. A way to be something." Jack said

"But what about the rest? If your right, he has some other people doing the same thing." Roger asked, wrestling with the life he had taken.

"How do you get a million Germans to hate the Jews?" Jack asked. "You make it the price of belonging. Everyone wants to belong. Everyone wants to make a connection. Jocks belong to the jocks, the drop outs who hate the establishment belong to the rest of the drop outs following the drop out code of hating "The man." Isis are experts at it, they collect the disenfranchised and promise them love and attention for hating America." Jack kept the phone to his ear while looking at Roger's blank face.

"You don't need to tell someone to shoot Trump you just have to make hating Trump the price of being how you get to be one of the cool kids. There will always be some useful idiot that does the unthinkable. Trump, Biden, Lincoln, doesn't matter." Jack paused thinking about what he had said.

"Adler would have no problem finding some lost souls to follow him. He probably could spot emotional zombies like him from miles away. Belonging is more important than fo...." Jack stopped. He scared himself realizing what was going to happen next.

"It's too late for an intervention." Jack said slowly. "He made that clear with his literal dying breath. We have to take him at his word. He wasn't stupid. It could be as simple as someone trying to call him and he doesn't answer. That alone just not answering the phone could trigger whatever he was planning." Each new aspect jack thought of convinced him that he was right.

Roger didn't know or understand the depth of Jack's conviction but he figured Adler was up to something big. Big enough to kill Darlene and Jack's dirty bomb was certainly big, so he accepted that Jack had to go.

"You better go." Roger said and Jack knew Roger was going to be okay.

"See you in a few days." Jack said knowing he still had several minutes to walk to the seven eleven he pinned for meeting the Uber driver.

"Roger, not that I am telling you what to say but Jennie has a point. Sometimes the less the police know the better." Jack said.

"I know." Roger said.

"No, I'm just saying let them build up some momentum before you tell them about Darlene." Jack said."Dirty bomb." Roger said. "I need to convince them that there is a dirty bomb without sounding crazy. This prick is wearing a Nazi uniform and I may end up looking like the nut. Fuck this." Roger said shaking his head and laughing at the situation.

Jack walked toward the door pad of paper in one hand two pens in his pocket. "Call homeland security. Make the report to both of them and don't tell them I flew out, just tell them I walked away. I don't need to get arrested when I land."

"Will do. This is a simple self-defense story; I confronted him about a string of murders I investigated. I confronted him and he pulled a gun on me. I tackled him, and he got shot. That is the simple truth." Roger said with a strong voice. Then he turned to Jack.

"Germantown boss." Roger said sticking out a hand.

Jack shook Rogers's hand and felt a firm shake. It would not mean much to people who didn't know Roger, but Jack understood. Roger didn't shake hands much, not a huggy high five guy.

They had been friends long enough for Jack to

understand. Despite everything, Roger was still solid.

"Touch base when you can. Push homeland security if anyone is going to take this seriously it's them." Jack said matching the confidence he felt in Roger's shake then quickly walked out the door toward the nothing he planned and the worst day of his life.

Chapter Twenty

Jack was in line to board the plane. To anyone who looked he was on vacation without luggage. The voice in his head was disgusted, muttering: "Seven hour flight with time change, rental cars, drive time, it all adds up. I must be stupid." Jack had gotten the only flight he could from LAX to Dulles International. He calculated time from his arrival to the Department of Energy building in Germantown Maryland. Eleven o'clock he thought, if I'm lucky. It was the only plan he had. The 911 attack was on his mind. They happened at about 9:11 AM. If Adler's Nazi's wanted to repeat 911, he would be too late.

As he began double checking the time calculations, he realized the 911 attack was based more on airlines schedules than some numerology. He relaxed a little frustrated that he did not know more about Adler's plan. He would have to fill in some blanks, maybe even make up a few things to get the DOE to take action. He hoped Roger could find some computer files but he knew they would be password protected at the least, probably encrypted.

Jack looked around at the endless lines. Waiting, life is full of useless waiting. He hated it. Everything takes time and he didn't have any to spare. It occurred to him that time is the only thing you can't make or buy but never stop spending. "That's not bad." He though as fatigue washed over him like a wave in the Pacific that he never got to see.

Jack needed to start putting all the details on paper. Maybe a plan would somehow appear to him. He had to do something anything was better than a blind call to Homeland Security. He might as well be reporting an alien abduction.

Jack looked at the other passengers, red eyed bargain hunters. Heart attacks in a sack in one hand, backpack or purse in the other. None of them knew they may be flying into the epicenter of a nuclear bomb.

He chuckled thinking that the portly guy wearing his best "I spill everything" shirt was a government employee. "Great." He thought. I walk into the DOE building and Portly Sloberman there takes a report which he sends it to his supervisor who sends it to his supervisor who puts it on a conference agenda and nine months from now they decide to do nothing.

It was a good moment to ponder if he had gotten carried away in a fiction of his own making, but Jack didn't go there. He still had enough energy to avoid the doom clouds that seeded his mind when he was young. Jack focused on his notes. Before the plane hit the runway he sketched out bullet points with facts and then looked at them shaking his head loud enough to make a few other passengers look at him. He realized he was in more trouble than he thought.

I walk in and say what "There is a guy planning to attack this building. He thinks he is the next Hitler, and he was wearing a Nazi uniform in Los Angeles. He is a probate lawyer; well actually he was because he is dead now." It sounded crazy and he saw it happen. A free ride to the gray bar motel. That's where I am going he thought.

They were probably somewhere over Nevada when he began searching the internet for information. Google maps had detailed pictures of the Department of Energy building in Germantown Maryland. The US Department of Energy web site gave a detailed history of the location. "How stupid are we." he thought, all this information open to anyone who wants and is willing to spend two seconds looking on their phone. Notes, more notes, and then re-writing the notes to make sure they made sense.

Jack was finishing the second round of notes underlining the one he thought was the most important, it's not what he said but how he said it that mattered. "I need to sleep." he thought fighting the urge to keep working on a plan that he couldn't make without sleeping. He put the pen down and looked at the pages and pages of scribbling. He knew it was not enough.

"Wow" he thought. "How can sleep sneak up on you like that?" He glanced up and saw the stewardess. "Pillow" she asked, reading his eyes, which anyone could have. "Please" he said as she handed him one and tucked another behind him. Jack slept quickly and better than he expected. He woke up feeling the familiar drop of the airplane's descent in his gut. Glancing out the window he knew he had time to go over the history and facts before calling Roger.

He glanced at his phone, six missed calls, all Roger, nothing from Jennie. That would have to wait, probably needed to make notes for her too. He shook his head, trying to wake up and start back on the next revision of his notes.

Follow the money he thought that made sense. He began to list the charities that kept coming up in Adler probate cases. He wrote down the ones he could remember. "New Hope a Veterans Charitable Trust," "Roth Chufeir French based charitable trust for children." He Goggled French charities and the name Chufeir, but didn't find anything meaningful. No time to play stupid Nazi code games. He wanted to call Roger to tell him he was alright but he was awake enough to realize that either Homeland Security or the Police probably had Roger's phone.

In addition to a wire tap they had his number and digital id's meant they could identify the cell tower he was using within seconds.

If he called they would know where he was and could have somebody waiting to arrest him when he got off the plane. Bad idea to call Roger so he started back on a new set of bullet points in a new order but images of being arrested as he walked off the plane were hard to avoid. He was tired, too tired. He reclined his seat and glanced for his little pillow but he didn't need it.

Jack woke up groggy because he had to put his seat in the upright position for landing. A few anxious minutes later he was walking off the plane eyes darting in every direction.

He expected to be arrested but there was no one there. Spotting a trash can he threw his notes away. "Worthless." He thought. "I got no plan." He decided to stop thinking about the facts. He glanced at his dirty jeans and figured he smelled worse than he looked. "Even if I had enough facts, it won't matter if I look like a homeless guy wearing a tin foil hat.

Time would be well spent if he stopped and bought a decent shirt, some shaving cream, a razor and all the usual stuff. Crazy people have day old beards wear foil hats and tell alien attack conspiracy stories. I will make a business like appearance. Maybe it will get me past the first gate.

He stopped at a Wal-Mart store after getting a rental car and driving far enough away from the airport to feel like he was not being followed. Good enough he thought. Two bags later and was taking a whores bath in the bathroom sink talking to himself in silence staring into a crappy mirror trying to shave. He tore the tags from a white dress shirt and shook the black jacket. He used the finger nail cutters he bought to cut the plastic tags off everything then decided he didn't need to trim his nails.

Hair slicked back and gelled enough to stick he looked at the results, "If you can't dazzle them with brilliance baffle them with bullshit." He said to no one. Man he thought I'm starting to sound like my grandpa.

Confident that he left the tin foil hat behind, he slid

into the rental car and turned the key. He looked at his phone. No new calls from Roger. Why the hell didn't he leave a message Jack thought suppressing his fear that the calls came from the police who had taken Rogers phone.

Jack looked down, the engine was running and he was ready to drive. It would not take long to get there, but Jennie was taking up space in the windshield. He had to do something or she would block his ability to think all day. He let out a long breath and tried to think about her. He smiled, and then typed a text. "Sorry I was not more support last night, I am in DC and need to stop this bomb." Before he finished typing "bomb" he started erasing what he typed.

I can't send that he thought, Jennie did not think there was a bomb. Why didn't she text him. Was she mad? Was it over? Jack sat trying to clear his mind. Fear always feeds the lonely animal. It was the worst. He wished Jennie was there but at the same time he was glad she wasn't. He put down his phone and started to drive listening for the next direction.

Chapter Twenty One

19901 Germantown Road, Germantown, Maryland was an older building. It was easy to find because the government always hires the lowest bidder and they always built the same simple crap. As expected, it was clean but without specific meaning or interest. Nothing you could see gave any clue about what may be inside.

Jack walked into the small lobby through what was obviously the front door. Glass walls and government grade tortilla thin carpet faded from age matching his expectations. The slightly over industrial grade furniture looked like something Reagan bought before he was the President. Security glass separated Jack from an attendant.

Glad they have security for an attack, hate that they have security keeping me out he thought. He was tired and his mind was wandering. A twenty something girl behind the partly open glass window look at him with a blank stare. She looked fit, clear brown eyes surrounded by bright white next to the slight natural tan of her skin. The look on her face was stern. "Resting bitch face" is a real thing but she didn't have it. Free from makeup, jack decided she was not really fit but not being fat in America made you appear fit. Her multi colored hair was a mix of various browns, black and maybe red looking strands.

It was twisted behind her head making her look serious. Jack knew the uniform was for a purpose but he also knew the uniform did not always match the attitude.

Jack reached to open that new lap top he purchased at Wal-Mart, which was empty then closed it and patted his chest pockets.

"I'm sorry I seem to have handed out all my cards. I'm Jack Alexander. I am a researcher senior for government affairs with the Rand Corporation." He paused to see if she would react. Nothing.

"We are a think tank studying latent effects of radiation and isotopes in post modern steal and beam construction. Jack scolded himself for stringing together too many buzz words that made him look suspect. "Post modern?" The voice in his head questioned. He and Jennie had watched some postmodern jukebox videos at the hotel when they were thinking about going to a karaoke joint so Jennie could sing. If naturally tan was into karaoke he just made a fool out of himself.

"I just flew in and I haven't had time to make an appointment. May I speak with the security manager on duty?" Jack said just as he rehearsed a dozen times in his head thinking "Please don't say "That's me."

"What's this about?" Gate girl asked her honest face serious like she was in formation at some remote army base.

"My firm does web search thereat and counter threat terrorism encryption and isolation using radioactive isotope tracing.

We have detected a credible and immediate threat to this facility and I just need to speak the security manager about it." It was garbage and Jack knew it. He hoped she didn't know it.

Despite knowing that he had said stupid things from the start Jack did not think fast enough to change anything. He was too tired and for the first time he though this whole idea may be a waste. She stared at him with little more than a blank look on her face.

Jack looked at her name tag, "Ruiz." He considered using her name remembering that using a person's name makes you appear more genuine but it was too late. Using her name now would just make him look manipulative and her guard was already up.

"Again I'm sorry I would have called for an appointment, but the chatter on the dark web is so active, I'm afraid there really wasn't time." Jack added thinking that for garbage; it wasn't bad No one really knew what the dark web was.

She squinted just a little trying to understand. Jack spotted it and decided to use it. If he could confuse her enough she might call for help. Then he remembered a trick for building trust when the police stop you while driving. Turn on the dome light and put your hands on the steering wheel facing the officer. When the police pull you over the best way to show that you are not a threat was through body language. Jack reached for his wallet as another guard walked up to the desk from the back.

"Here is my driver's license, and again I am sorry that I ran out of cards." Jack said thinking he should have started that way. Jack looked at the new guard.

"I just need to speak with the security supervisor about a threat to this facility that my firm discovered after a very long investigation. Unfortunately it is very time sensitive." Jack slowed his speech a little and tried to make his voice sound confident. How do you sound confident when you are going to tell a story that will make you look nuts?

The new guard was middle aged with short cropped hair that looked like it would have been a respectable flat top when he was younger. A moustache and glasses made him look a bit serious. He had no markings on his shirt that made him look more important than Ms. Ruiz but it was clear he was in charge, or more in charge than she was.

Davis was the name on his tag, or something like that and he had a gun strapped to his waist. Armed security always cost more. The fact that the government paid for it meant there was something in the building worth protecting. Davis looked at Jack's license and turned to make a copy of it. "Start a contact card." He said to Ruiz still seated behind her desk.

Davis grabbed a "Visitor-Escort Required" badge from a board behind Ruiz and waited while the computer imported a copy of his license to the contact card. Jack wanted to talk smooth things over but feared he would somehow screw up his "Visitor status." It was smarter to keep quiet. He tried to look smart, but didn't know how.

Grabbing a clip board, Davis disappeared into the

back only to open the side door a few seconds later. Davis was chunky. He looked and moved in a lazy fashion. Clip board in one hand, visitors tag in the other, large radio stuffed into a back pocket, Jack suspected that high school football was his peak. He never stopped eating the five thousand calorie's he put away when he ran and tacked people for a few hours a day.

"Come this way please." Davis said, holding the door so Jack could grab it at the same time he was handing him the badge. Jack bumped the door with his butt and grabbed the badge with his free hand, the other wrapped around his new bag. Jack clipped the badge to his chest pocket and followed Davis through the door.

"Sorry if I am slow our firm has been working on this so much it's like back when I had two a days." Jack said confident that Davis would relate to him having two practices in one day.

"No problem" Davis said in a friendly tone.

Davis took Jack down a hallway then turned into another hallway. Jack suspected he was in a main hallway because the crappy carpet had a clear dirt and wear pattern down the middle. If there was nuclear waste at this facility there would be lots of inspections and that could wear out a cheap carpet fast. Just before a set of unlocked double doors, Davis opened a side door inside of which was a conference table. He motioned to Jack saying "Have a seat."

The room looked like a million other meeting rooms or perhaps older rooms because there was no monitor or electronics, just an old phone. No windows just the one door and a single table in the middle. "At least I made it past the front door." Jack thought.

Davis stood at the door looking down the hallway. He heard a noise from the double doors and turned, saying "There you are." Jack was hopeful it was the head of security, but knew he was wrong when a teenager came into the room.

Acne red splotches marks randomly dotting his white cheeks he was wearing the same uniform as everyone else. The shirt was creased like it was new. Jack noticed there was no name tag. Jittery and nervous, the kid did not stand still. A radio was clipped to his belt, microphone on his shoulder lapel.

Jack took out a note pad and two pens, setting them on the table. He put the lap top to his right but didn't open it because he did not want them to ask what was on it.

Davis placed the clip board in front of the kid. "Ready?" He asked.

"Yes sir."

"Great." Jack thought, "I got a trainee." He saw a clear tape name tag that looked like it came from a printer. He guessed it was temporary. "Russell."

"My name is Jack Alexander. Do you want me to spell that?" Jack asked knowing Russell would say yes.

"A-l-e-x, a-n-d, er. Jack avoided the military style of stating the word associated with the letters feeling time pressing against the back of his neck.

"Use the contact card." Davis told Russell pointing.

Jack tried to wait but he was too impatient and too tired to wait long. He looked at Davis.

"I have discovered a well funded plan to attack this facility and steal some of the classified materials that are stored here." Start with the easy stuff. He looked at Russell. He was writing. Well, actually he was printing and not very fast.

"The plot was started by a group of radical terrorists headed by a man named Adler. They plan to attack the United States at one or more major population areas inflicting wide scale damage, more than likely simultaneously."

Jack spoke with confidence and it showed. "Now I have their attention." He thought.

"What kind of population areas?" Davis asked.

"I am not sure of the exact locations, but New York and D.C. are high on the list." Jack said but he scolded himself for saying "I" instead of "we" because he knew "we" made him sound less crazy.

"We identified several targets but unfortunately we do not know the order of the attacks. Given the urgency we felt it was better to meet with you folks right away." Jack was pleased with his presentation.

"Do I write that down?" Russell asked.

"Yeah." Davis said, giving him a stupid look.

"He said he wasn't sure." Russell said.

"Were taking a statement, if he says he is not sure,

that is his statement, so that is what we write down." Davis responded. "Great." Jack thought I am being used for training.

"Listen, is there someone else I should be talking to." Jack pushed just as the door opened.

"John." Said an unknown man poking his head in the door, "Can I talk to you?"

Jack couldn't see who was at the door because he was facing the other way but he was hopeful it was good news. He twisted in his seat just as the door was closing. Davis exited and Jack was alone with Russell. He sat there in silence. Trying to think of what he could say that would make them call their boss. Looking crazy would get him shuffled out the door and there would be no second chance. The door opened and Davis walked back into the room.

Behind him was a middle aged man, short hair, fit and wearing a cheap tie that didn't match his two day old beard, if you could call two days a beard. He did not bother to introduce himself. "Middle management has arrived this is going nowhere." Jack thought.

Davis looked alert. He took the clip board from Russell, "Okay," he said handing it back, in a curt manner.

"You said there is a threat to this facility. What have you got on that?"

"My group identified a well funded cell of terrorists who are going to steal material from this facility. We don't have bank records back yet, but we estimate they have millions in financial backing and because of the finances we expect the attack will be well coordinated." Jack paused. He didn't want to get to the important part until he had built up some credibility. Jack looked at Russell who was still writing. He did not wait for him to finish.

"The timing of the attack is my primary concern. We believe it could happen as early as today, but in any case no later than the end of this week." Jack spoke with confidence, even though he was not sure.

"What is the name of the group?" Davis asked.

"We have not given them a name and we hesitate to name groups who do not self identify."

Jack thought that was a good line. They are nationals and their leader is a neo Nazi but I cannot emphasize enough that we avoid labels because that often obscures important details." Jack felt good about his approach. They did not respond.

"Gentleman," Jack said his voice a little louder pausing for effect. "The terrorists plan to steal nuclear waste and make a dirty bomb." There it was. He had to give them the ultimate punch line and they had nothing to say. There was no reaction. Jack was hoping the mention of nuclear material would get the guards excited. They acted like they had never heard the word nuclear. He waited as long as he dared, then decided to repeat the punch line. Was there something wrong with these guys?

"You do understand." He said staring at Davis

intently. "This is as serious as it gets. Perhaps you should bring in a manager and we can check on things." Jack offered.

"How do you spell nuclear?" Russell asked Davis.

"Just right it down any way, we can fix it later." Davis said, Jack looked at Davis, and just then realized that Davis had given the clipboard back to Russell. Giving the clipboard back to the trainee was a clear sign. He could almost see a reflection of his tin foil hat in Davis's glasses. He was losing.

"No." Jack said out of frustration looking at Davis. "You better spell it right 'N-u-c-l-e-a-r' as in 'clear,' which I don't think I am making myself." Jack paused, "This is very serious business." He added trying not to raise his voice.

"Oh, we know it is." Davis said dismissing him.

"I don't think you do." Jack said, intentionally glaring at Davis. Perhaps starting a fight was a better idea. There was no response. Maybe it was too late.

"Do you have any idea how many pounds of spent nuclear waste you have here." Jack said ready to bluff.

"There's none of that here sir, sorry." Davis said like a teacher in an elementary school. Jack was certain he was losing. He could feel the clock ticking on his visitors pass. Russell, had stopped writing, and he swallowed hard to avoid yelling at them because he knew that would punch his ticket to the door.

"Sir," Jack said trying to command the room. "I want your report to be perfect, because I can and quite frankly I will use it to show that the facility was warned before the attack if nothing else." Jack was staring intently at Davis, hoping maybe he could scare him into getting his boss.

"Should I write that down?" Russell asked.

"No, don't write that down." Davis said, calling Jack's bluff.

"But you told me to document what happened." Russell said

"Just put down threat to security....no wait put down insult." Davis said, fighting back against Jack's threat.

"No." Jack said, "Write down Terrorists stealing Plutonium."

Russell started to write but paused. "Pluto, like the dog" Jack said. "Nium."

"It doesn't....Just put down fifty one fifty." Davis said not looking at Jack.

Jack did not know what fifty one fifty meant. He had somehow missed the California counter culture that took pride in having experienced a Health and Safety Code Section 5150 mental health hold. The law allowed the police to detain people that may be a danger to themselves or others for 72 hours. It was a modern day drunk tank. A badge of honor that showed you "partied to the max." The police used it generically as an icon for crazy.

"You are making a judgment call." Jack said figuring "5150" was a conclusion about him that sank his credibility. If you were going to fight, might as well do it with bare knuckles Jack thought,

"When they are looking for someone to blame your conclusions will put you at the top of the list." Davis just looked at him.

"Look, I am not trying to be a jerk." Back to being "Mr. Reasonable" Jack thought since the Neanderthal flexing was not working.

"I am sure my boss is calling your boss but it will take a lot of time for the information to filter down. A guy named Adler died yesterday and that is a trigger that limits the time we have. I don't want lives lost while we wait for bureaucrats to beef up security." Calm and solid, Jack was doing everything he could. There was a pause.

"No reason to worry, we are plenty beefed up here." Davis said.

"Really?" Jack asked, but caught himself before he argued knowing it would extend the flex fight.

"I'm not saying you have a Demon Core here, but I don't see sufficient security for the amount of Plutonium 239, you have, or is it 238?" Jack was bluffing that they did not know what was behind the locked doors and that uncertainty might make them call someone who might know.

"Make the call." Tie man said from behind Jack. Jack turned. He had forgotten that the tie man was there. As he turned he saw the tie man had jumped up and was exiting the room at speed.

"What?" Davis asked. Looking at tie man headed out the door. "Why?"

"Because he is the smartest guy in the room and he knows things you don't." Jack said indulging his caveman impulses to punch Davis.

Tie man was out the door as he yelled "Code 99" over his shoulder to Davis.

Davis slowly pulled the radio from his pocket and turned up the volume bringing it to his face.

"Radio check, all sectors, I have a code 99." The radio cracked to life. "Sector six Jimenez here, read you loud and clear."

A voice reported with a slight accent they could not place. Davis turned the volume down after several voices came on the radio to respond with "okay," "Roger" "A-okay" and similar. "Satisfied?" Davis asked, looking at Jack.

"No." Jack said. That wasn't Jimenez.

Davis stared at him. .

"Jimenez is a Spanish name." Jack said. "But he said *Ji-menez*, which just about all of us know is wrong. It's *Hi-menez*." There was a pause. "So who was it?" Jack asked.

Russell stood up and said "I got it." Davis looked at Jack and squinted a little trying to remember what Jimenez said. He was staring at Jack like they were arm wrestling. Jack locked eyes back refusing to blink.

A massive bang slammed Jack's right side. Startled, he folded to his left trying to make himself smaller. Davis' light blue shirt turned dark red and his face went blank. He let go of the radio and slumped to his right slowly falling to the floor. Jack stared his ears ringing like he was in a bad dream where reality wasn't real.

"Code G." Russell said speaking into his radio gun in his right hand pointing straight at Jack.

Jack didn't think. He stared at the gun then up at Russell. Nothing more than a kid, not even twenty. Jack was frozen hands slightly in the air from before when he was covering from the long bang. Jack struggled to understand what he was seeing. The kid was too young to hate, and far too young to kill. Could Adler's computer really know what appealed to lost kids and then manipulate them to join bizarre causes? Russell looked at Jack's blank face.

Jack's shoulders dropped. He was too stunned to realize what his subconscious already knew. His last thought would be that he lost. He lost because he couldn't figure out how extreme people could get. How do you get normal Germans to hate Jews….he knew the answer but he failed because he did not see how Adler's computer saw it, understood it and used it to manipulate lost souls. AI was going to kill us all with human fools but the blood was really on the hands of the people who used it to manipulate the masses expecting some gain.

The radio cracked startling Jack. "Force on 10." Russell walked backwards to the door never moving his eyes from Jack. He reached behind him and swung the door open slipping outside then pulled the door closed.

Jack was confused. He pushed himself up from the table and peered over at Davis' body. "How the hell did I get here?" Jack stood not moving. He listened trying to see if he could hear gun fire. There was nothing. Jack looked up to the ceiling hoping to see tiles he could remove, but the ceiling was solid.

I brought this on myself he thought. Why the hell did I think I could somehow save things? He remembered the phrase "Run hide fight." Hide wasn't an option Russell knew he was there. He glanced around the room to see if there was enough furniture to barricade the door but he knew there wasn't.

He looked at the door, no lock. He listened but heard nothing. He opened the door and peaked out. He saw nothing. Stay or run, fight didn't sound good. He took two steps and looked at Davis's body. "I'm sorry Man." He said out loud. "I should have stayed in California, and then you would still be alive." Without knowing he had made a decision Jack opened the door peeked out and saw no one. He reversed the path he followed when he came in.

He did not see anyone but he still rushed and to his surprise adrenaline shoved the gas pedal faster than made sense until he was surrounded by traffic.

Chapter Twenty Two

Assistant Secretary Jeremy Baker walked into the no-name burger joint carrying a white shopping bag with a store logo on it Jack didn't recognize. It seemed to weigh very little. He looked at the staff behind the counter then turned to walk down the aisle where Jack and Roger were sitting. It looked like he had been there before, he knew the place. Jack suspected as much because he let Baker pick it. Baker was wearing Khaki's a black belt that matched his slip on dress shoes with a light blue collared polo looking shirt under a navy blue Eisenhower jacket zipped half way up. It wasn't cold enough for a jacket Jack thought so he looked for a revolver sized bulge on his side but couldn't find one. Baker was smarter than to let it show.

Jet black hair parted on the side, not a single one out of place. His shave was so close it looked like he never needed to shave. As Baker got closer Roger moved to sit next to Jack. Baker slid into the booth opposite them and Jack smelled a faint scent of bar soap.

Unlike three days before when Jack had not known who he was, calling him "tie man," Jack was sure that Baker was a cop, head on a swivel surveying everything as he made his way to sit across from them.

"Gentlemen." He said sitting with rigid posture angled to see the room.

"Sorry about asking you to keep things quiet, but I had to write the report and brief the uh, powers that be."

"I don't think we actually meet." Jack offered.

"Jeremy." He said extending a hand. Jack shook it. Jeremy glanced at Roger but he knew there would be no hand shake. Roger didn't trust him.

Jeremy Baker was a man who understood power and he knew he had it. Power makes you polite. It makes you smile because you know, in the end, you get your way. Roger had trusted that type of smile before only to be "back stabbed" as he put it. A stab that left a scar on Roger that had not healed. Jack accepted it as part of what made Roger, well Roger.

"What's with all the secrecy?" Jack asked before Roger could start. "There wasn't anything on the news about this."

Baker smiled, "There were a few stories, but the web is pretty big and not everyone searches very deep into odd ball stories. Nothing to worry about."

Roger started to speak. But Jack knew it was smarter to interrupt him. "Odd ball? What I don't get is why the DOE has what I am guessing was a lot of 239?" Baker looked at Jack, and Jack knew he was sizing him up. Fine, Jack thought I will back it up.

"I get the history; DOE was created at the end of WWII specifically to handle nuclear material. They were not subject to the same regulations as DOD so they could experiment with yields. They were trying to produce the most deadly nuclear weapons possible. All those tests at Bikini Island and in Nevada were all without or with very little oversight. Regardless, it sure wasn't the Nuclear Regulatory Agency…" Jacks voice trailed. It always did when he was thinking faster than he could speak.

Baker couldn't tell looking at Jack if he had figured it out, but he knew it was a good time to offer an explanation.

"The DOE follows NRC safety guidelines and regulations. NASA needs 238, so they 'wash down,' if you will, 239." He did not pause. He was studying them more than thinking of what he would say.

"That's what they used to power the Mars rover, and other extraterrestrial vehicles. DOE provides it. What you saw was nothing more than a disgruntled employee who voiced a lot of displeasure and threats. He was apprehended by DOE security."

"Disgruntled?" Roger said. "Bullshit. That wasn't one disgruntled employee." Jack looked at Roger and then back at Baker. "I don't know what you heard but we are no different than any other employer.

We have disgruntled employees from time to time, just like private companies." Baker said with a confident tone.

"That's complete crap and you know it." Roger said more calm that Jack expected.

"Roger," Jack said. "They don't care. They don't have to disclose the 238. They probably got it from a burned out Russian reactors. The stuff we made in Georgia was all buried to save the environment years ago. All those nuclear statutes and regulation books we saw in Adler's office, Title Ten of the Federal Code.

The Department of Energy is not the military it is the perfect place to hide nuclear material. They probably have enough to wipe out half the nation." Jack paused looking at Baker.

"What were you doing there?" Jack asked for the first time trying to understand who Baker was.

"Routine inspection." Baker answered.

"How routine, weekly, monthly, quarterly." Jack pried.

Baker looked at Jack with a slight smile. Power also means you do not have to explain.

"As often as needed." Baker said. Jack didn't laugh, but he couldn't help expelling air suppressing a laugh. It made him look like he didn't believe Baker which Baker already knew.

"You're fuckin' telling me we stumble onto a plot to steal a shit load of radioactive nuclear crap and spread all over America killing millions and this ass is gonna tell people it was a disgruntled employee and there was nothing nuclear there." Roger said to Jack.

Baker did not smile, "The evidence is quite clear. The police reports are being reviewed by senior management as we speak. You can probably put in a FOIA request and get them in a month or so." Baker said.

Roger looked at Jack. He did not know what a FOIA request was. Jack knew it stood for "Freedom of Information Act" and he also knew the government used it to hide things they wanted secret like material from the Kennedy assassination. You have a right to request anything but they drag it out and in the end they always won.

Roger looked at Jack like he wanted to argue. Jack knew how to end it.

"The house always stands on 16." It was a reference to many conversations they had about gambling and how much money Vegas makes on the game 21. Even though the player knows the house stands on 16, they still lose.

Jack hoped Roger would understand that he would lose pushing the truth any further than Baker would let it be known.

"Our security is the best in the nation." Baker offered. "It should be no surprise that we were able to identify a disgruntled employee who took his own life in a struggle with authorities." It was a well planed comment.

"You're full of crap." Roger said an automatic reaction after a week of bad news that had him tired of being jerked around.

"No, I'm full of patriotism, and you are too." Baker said staring at Roger. "You wouldn't have called us unless you were a patriot. No one would have come to Maryland knowing what you, think you knew unless you were a patriot."

"Patriot my ass. Patriots tell the truth." Roger said.

"No doubt." Baker said, as if he knew what Roger was going to say, "But it is still illegal to yell fire in a

crowded theater. Even freedom of speech gives way to the greater public good in certain situations."
Washington double speak, power on display. It was as close to an admission as they would get.

"Are you telling me I have to keep my mouth shut about this? That's bullshit; I am going to tell anyone and everyone I damn well want too and there aint a damn thing you can do to stop me." Roger barked at Baker, the hair on his spine rising like an angry dog.

Baker was nodding in agreement. Jack understood what Baker was doing. When Baker glanced at him Jack could nearly read his mind and realized it would be better for Roger if it came from him.

"He doesn't need to." Jack said with a slight turn to his friend. "Tell whoever you want, but you might as well do it from the grassy knoll."

Roger looked at Jack. They had spent plenty of time talking about the JFK assassination so Roger understand that the more he talked about crazy things the more he would look crazy. The truth did not matter as much as what people thought was true. The more extreme the truth the more it looks like a lie. One post to social media and government bot farms would label him a conspiracy theorist to destroy any credibility he may have. Game over. Control the information; control the people, Washington played the game well.

Baker wanted to make sure the point was made.

"Are you planning an expedition to look for big foot Roger?" He asked with a soft voice.

Roger didn't laugh. He would take it from Jack but not Baker.

"If I did, I would find him." Roger said over an icy stare. Baker knew had gone too far.

"I have no doubt." Baker said. He locked eyes with Roger.

"Adler's death has been ruled a justified self defense. The District Attorney has already signed off on it. The case is closed so you have plenty of time for hunting or whatever you like Roger." Baker watched as Roger's his eyes grew huge. He knew Roger didn't know and he wanted to watch his reaction. Power got things done and Baker was displaying the power he had. Roger was so shocked he had nothing to say.

"I can't stay long but I do have something for you." Baker said opened the plastic bag. "By the way, we are putting out a new job announcement on USA Jobs. We are looking for some intelligence analysts with broad analytical skills. Prior law enforcement is a plus." Then he stopped pulling at whatever was in the bag and froze for a moment looking at Roger to make his point.

"Irregularities in a person's service history wouldn't be a problem." Then turning to look at Jack he added, "Someone with an insider's view of criminal proceedings even if they were once accused of some crime would not be a disqualifier so long as they had a pardon or something like that."

Roger's jaw dropped a little, but Jack forced his face to go blank. He didn't want Baker to have the satisfaction of having two up on them.

Baker smiled then continued opening the bag. "Just something to think about." He pulled two cardboard covered long blue felt boxes out of the bag and checked the number on one end sliding it to Jack. He handed the other to Roger somehow knowing Roger would take it but as planned Baker did not let go forcing Roger to look at him so he could smile and let Roger know that this was big.

"We are truly grateful." Baker said.

"What is it?" Roger asked, pulling the blue box out of the cardboard and flipping up the lid.

"It is a Presidential Medal of Freedom." Baker said, in a tone he reserved for serious times.

"Really?' Roger said, honestly surprised.

"Congratulations." Baker said flatly.

Jack opened the box and saw a red white and blue ribbon holding a bronze medal embossed with a seal. He didn't take it out of the box.

"What no hearty handshake?" Roger snapped not willing to give up being pissed off. "Or are you savin' that for the ceremony."

"This is it." Baker said, "Sorry, no band." Shaking his head in a firm manner that would convince most the conversation was over.

"Are you kidding, what is this shit? First you say nothing happened then we get a medal that's bullshit." Roger said voice rising. He looking around for someone he might involve in his brewing rage. Baker didn't say anything. It took a smart person to know when not speaking was making the loudest point, and Baker was plenty smart.

Roger stared at Baker. "Nothing to say?" Voice lowered to normal.

"National Security." Jack said.

"I'm glad you understand." Baker responded, a rehearsed line.

"Understand what?" Roger said. "I don't get it. I don't get anything."

Baker looked at Jack, but Jack was not going to bail him out.

Baker looked at Roger,

"That means, nobody knows. Grateful as the president is, we will keep this private to protect national security." Baker was using his official stern, confident voice.

"You're shitting me." Roger said.

"No, he's not." Jack said, before Baker could talk. "And that explains our meeting in…." Jack paused looked around finally understanding why Baker picked no name burger in no name suburb.

"What is this place anyway?" Jack asked, circling a finger so Baker could understand the question. Baker gave Jack a small smile so Jack would know he was right. Baker had picked a quiet public place so they would behave and there was no record of the meeting. Scream if they wanted, Baker would walk out and it would be as if they never meet.

Jack looked up and saw security cameras. He looked down at Baker who had not turned around but still knew what Jack was looking for.

"They're dummies, but they work. This place hasn't been robbed in years."

Jack laughed. "Let me guess, the report is in a fifty year file somewhere."

"I like you Jack." Baker said, broadening his smile to a genuine but controlled extent. He appreciated that Jack quickly understood what was happening.

"I like you too Roger, but for a whole different set of reasons." Baker said more genuine than Roger cared to consider. All Roger heard was Baker giving him a phony pat on the back.

Jack chuckled; an unconscious reaction to the realization that he had done everything Baker knew he would do before he walked into the place.

"What are you telling us? Roger said that we get a phony medal and you bury the whole thing."

Roger asked pitching the medal on the table. He wanted Baker to lay it out.

"The medals are real." Baker said, but the records about why they were awarded are not public at this time." Baker said.

"It's like the JFK files they released 50 years after he was shot – sort of. Makes me wonder though." Jack said squinting one eye as he tilted his head to the side and looked at Baker. "What exactly is going on at the Department of Energy?"

"Going on?" Baker repeated, slight emphasis on the word going, it was enough for Jack to finish the thought.

"Nothing now I suppose." Smart Jack thought, move the operation to prevent another incident and help deny anything happened. Baker smiled. Jack didn't want to like him but he did. Baker sat up in the bench and moved his weight ready to stand.

"In, fifty years." He said, tipping a hand toward Jack so they would understand that his earlier guess about the sealed files was right. "The report will become public and people are going to know how much your efforts meant."

Baker did not smile. He had said all he was going to say. He wadded up the bag. A subtle body language trick he used to sub consciously signal the end of the conversation. Two seconds later he stood.

Jack smiled; he knew there was no reason to debate or rather no point in trying.

"This is bullshit." Roger said.

"It comes from the top, I don't make these decisions. But I assure you." Baker said in a personal tone. "These medals have serial numbers, and I guarantee you the files are very clear. You are going to be quite pleased with it."

"Very top, huhn." Roger quipped. "Then let the fucking President come give these to us. Darlene is dead, and noting in your fucking fifty year file is going to change that, or make a God damned bit of difference for her kid." Roger could take losing but not in a rigged fight.

"I know." Baker said with a genuine nod of his head. They understood that his comment was personal. Then he repeated it, "I know." It sank in.

Roger knew there was nothing he could do, but he didn't like how unfair it all felt. It was just wrong. He wanted to yell, he wanted to punch someone but there was no one left to blame.

Baker had paused ready to return Rogers next exasperated comment to help him understand and accept what had to be but it never happened. He knew not to smile.

5,6,7. Baker was counting in his mind, seven seconds was the number where experience taught him he could make a clean exit. He turned as planned then turned back.

"Take care of yourselves." his planned last words. He wanted them to be personal, final and soothing. Jack didn't know it was planned it felt genuine.

Baker walked to a spotless white Ford Explorer. He drove away as if nothing had ever happened.

"No one is ever going to read the report." Roger said feeling sorry for himself. He closed the lid of the blue felt box and sat quietly reflecting on what happened and how he got there. Jack left his metal on the table and slowly drank his iced tea from a straw till it made the empty gurgling sound.

Nothing was said other than Roger talking to

himself as he smiled and looked at memories and dreams he hoped to live with Darlene. Roger suddenly turned to Jack who was still sitting next to him as if he was startled to see him.

"I need a vacation. Just a week or so I have to back to LA."

"See you then." Jack said, happy that Roger seemed to have pointed the toes of his boots in a new direction.

"Thanks" Roger said already moving to stand.

Roger disappeared before Jack had finished thinking about what he was going to do. He needed to call Jennie. He was not sure what happened. He would have to admit that he had gotten lost in an obsession. He would tell her what happened and hoped she would understand. He would show her the medal and hope she didn't think he bought it at a DC souvenir shop. It was time to focus, really focus on her for a while. He probably couldn't make her understand but he would go to Dallas and let her lead for a while maybe get his life on track. He looked at the uneaten burger on the tray and picked it up but it was too cold and he wasn't hungry.

He stood up looking for a trash can to dump it. He was two steps toward the can next to the door when he saw a middle aged black man, short hair clean shirt and complexion sitting with his face half toward to the ceiling, eyes closed. "Prayer?" Jack thought, that's nice but it look odd.

"Are you alright?" Jack asked stopping with his

plastic tray in hand puzzled at what he saw.

The man lowered his chin and looked at Jack through blank eyes bathed in tears that hadn't spilled.

"My wife is mi…missing." He said, stumbling through a shaky voice clearing his throat.

"Did she work at…." Jack started, and then realizing his mistake, he sat down. "Tell me what happened?"

Chapter Twenty Three

Roger's timing was always poor, but he didn't care. He would have sat for as long as it took. Waiting was just part of his mission. He saw Gabriel exit the school and turn onto the side street headed to his grandmother's house. Roger knew he would find him there. "Straight to Grandma's good kid" he said out loud. He waited until Gabriel was next the passenger window of the curb parking he waited for earlier.

"Gabriel." Roger said, as the boy reached the door of the rented Ford. Gabriel glanced and his face lit up with surprise.

"Roger, what are you doing here? My dad said you weren't going to come around anymore." Gabriel said.

"I wanted to give you something." Roger said picking up the small white box from his passenger seat. He handed it to Gabriel through the open window. "This is from your Mom." He said.

"What did she get me? Gabriel asked looking like he hoped to tear it open and find a toy.

"It's not something she got you, it is something she did. She was a great lady and someday, when you are really old, you can open this box and read all about it." Roger said. Gabriel had a confused look on his face. Roger pointed to the top where he carefully taped his typed note. Read for yourself, it says:

"Gabriel, you will spend your whole life working, but when you are old, on the day you retire, open this box. It will tell you about your past, and how your mother was a great woman. Then you can tell your kids and grandkids about your courageous Mother." Gabriel followed as Roger read it.

"Put this at your grandma's house and forget about it. Years from now you will see it and then you will be proud of your Mom." Roger said staring intently into the little boys eyes.

"Gabriel come on." A boy yelled from the corner missing his chance to cross as the light turned yellow.

"Okay" Gabriel said tucking the small box into his backpack looking back toward his friends.

"Remember." Roger said in a stern voice that caused Gabriel to freeze. "Put it away. Wait until you are an old man. Yes?" Roger said, trying to imprint his plan into Gabriel's mind.

"Okay" Gabriel said turning to run to his friends. Roger was sure he would do it. He watched as Gabriel caught his friends, the box already forgotten. He felt a deep sense of calm. A satisfaction he could not identify. It eased the anger he still felt but he didn't think it was behind him. There was no tri-folded flag. No-one played taps. Carmen Maria Darlene Diaz was cremated forgotten by most of the world, but her story wouldn't end in a file that no one would ever open or care about. It would be a living thing carried by her son who would someday understand why she was killed.

His phone rang but he didn't look at it. He knew it was Jack. He hit answer on the steering wheel of the suburban he retrieved from long term parking when he flew East chasing Jack as he watched Gabriel disappear into a sun soaked web of California concrete.

"I'm still on vacation." Roger said.

"I know, but I need you to come back to DC when you're done.

The End

Honey for the Bear.

The alarm rolled through the room and over the covers like an earthquake that builds as it creeps closer. She regretted picking a rude tone because it was irritating its way through the center of her forehead like an emotional rug burn. Her eyes blinked open but closed quickly in a failed attempt to ignore the alarm.

January reached out and hit her phone hoping for the snooze button. She missed and had to pull herself away from gravity's embrace to stop the alarm causing her to fall to her feet taking the first awkward step of the day. She leaned forward nearly losing her balance quickly thrusting her right foot forward to catch herself. Lean walking all the way to the shower in the cold morning air she glanced back silently cursing the month she was named after.

Jeremy was still asleep tucked warm and unaware there was life outside his human crepe. She shook her head partly because she shivered and partly because of him. Another night butt to butt, another fight that left her frost butted. She hated that she had a name for it.

Shower then a clean uniform. Clean because she made it clean. A glance at the fresh snow out the window meant she was eating in the car again. Even with her wonderful all wheel drive Toyota it would take extra time to get to the hospital. Microwave perfection but no clean plates, 'I should have known" she thought.

"You're a slob." She yelled at him the night before. True as it was, he 'objected' to the tone.

"Endless nagging." The nerve of that man. He had no idea how little she nagged compared to how often she wanted too. "Endless Mess" she shot back in the same tone as his. The only way they could run out of plates with just the two of them was because he refused to clean the kitchen, or anything else for that matter.

The fight was over spilled coffee but really it wasn't. She spilled Coffee on her last clean uniform, trying to avoid tripping on a bucket full of some Triumph motorcycle parts. He was rebuilding something in the living room because it was too cold in the garage. "Who does that?" She asked an accusation more than a question.

"I didn't make you trip watch where you're going." Jeremy said. Bad idea…poke the Bear, see where that gets you and off they went.

"How hard is it?" She kept asking, pointing out half dozen 'slobisms' he didn't take care of. The dishes, the laundry, the refrigerator, the coffee maker, and now a bucket of crap that stinks.

"What the hell is that smell?" She asked but it was not a question. All he heard was "You are a stinking worthless slob."

"Carb. cleaner. It's the only thing that works." He said

"Works?" she shot back. "Great. You can ride to

work tomorrow in the snow."

"First off, I didn't bring the whole bike in. Second, I have to get it fixed now so I can ride it when the weather gets good."

"You don't listen."

"I do listen."

Silence followed except for the frustrated voice in her head. Despite setting the thermostat to sixty eight the frosty butts lasted until morning.

She tried to keep her mind on work it would help her ignore the fight. It was hard to focus creeping along in a single line of slow traffic. She took a solid breath of cool fresh air to shake off the mood as she entered the nearly silent emergency room happy to be at work where she had control.

"Hi January." Carmen said in a weary tone after a long night.

"The storm is bad. We have half a dozen call offs. Thanks for coming in."

"Sure," January said glancing around to see how many patients were in the ER.

"There is no one in family services, and it's your turn." Carmen said a mix of sympathy and certainty.

January hated the hospitals decision to implement "Full Family Services." She was not alone nearly the whole staff was in rebellion but they had not gotten far. Short staffed and already in a bad mood she let go of the desire to complain grabbed a clip board and turned to walk down the hall.

Family Services was the sad job of trying to take care of surviving family members whenever there was a death. She was part of the rotation if psychological services was overloaded, or like today short staffed. The hospital gave eight hours training and had picked nurses based on the idea that next step of grieving after denial, was "why" and nurses were the logical choice to explain the medical reasons why a person passed away. She hated it because sitting around meant long slow days. Figuring out what was wrong with patients and guessing what the doctor would order was the fun part of the job.

January stop and turned because Carmen wanted to give her some details. "Mary Burk. She died about three AM. Seventy-eight, MI, paramedics brought her in asystolic, so we didn't work her that long. Husband is Peter, didn't seem that surprised, but you know how that goes."

Carmen turned and January knew that meant the conversation was over. She braced herself and put on a somber face turning to walk down the hall. Somber came easy after the night she had with Jeremy. She loved him but it did not feel like love was enough.

Mary Burke lay on the emergency room gurney sheet pulled to her shoulders. The IV and heart monitor had been removed. She was waiting for a physician to finish the death certificate and decide if an autopsy was required. Peter Burke sat in a chair next to her with a blank look on his face.

Peter was a slender shriveled man with short gray

hair thinned enough to see his blotchy scalp. Light brown eyes that looked a little red more from a lack of sleep than from crying. His skin was wrinkled from a life of sun exposure and recent weight loss caused by a disease he had not spoke about with anyone other than his doctor.

"Hello, I'm January. I'm a staff nurse are you Mr. Burke?" January offered in a business tone as she was taught.

"Yes. Peter, please."

"Do you have any questions, or is there anything I can help you with?" January offered.

"No. Thank you." Peter said. "We were expecting this. She had been sick for quite some time." Peter turned to look at his deceased wife. There was a pause. January was expecting questions but there were none. She remembered a suggestion from her training designed to start conversation.

"How did you two meet?" January asked.

"I was mowing the lawn at a synagogue. She was walking down the street and said it looked good. I smiled but I was afraid to talk to her. Later that day I saw her at Simpsons Feed Store. The pigs were squealing so I went to see what the problem was. There she was trying to pick up a pig. You can't touch them. I said. Well why not? She asked." Peter smiled and paused re living the memory in his mind.

"She was so mad. They're too big. I told her. You have to pick them up from day one or they don't like it."

Peter looked at January and she could see a joy in his eyes.

"These are farm pigs.' I told her you just need to fatten them up. She got up mad as a wet hen looked at the little pigs and said serves you right, besides I like bacon better." Peter laughed thinking of his angry young wife.

"I suppose you think that's a sin or something. She said looking at me. I just stood there trying to figure out how it would be a sin to like bacon. It's not a sin I told her and then we just started talking about all kinds of things." Peter smiled. January could see that he was still in the feed store. He has a great memory she thought. She was thinking of another question to ask when Peter sat down next to her.

"She thought I was Jewish from the mowing job. I had no idea what being Jewish meant so I just kept asking her stupid questions. Finally she said you don't sound like most Jewish people I know. I'm Baptist. I told her and I'm sure I had a stupid look on my face because she got all upset. Well why the hell didn't you say anything she yelled at me. It was so funny. We laughed about it for years."

"That sounds nice." January said. Peter leaned back in his chair and crossed his legs.

"About a week later I went to a dance down at the Catholic Church. She went with friends and was sitting there when I walked in. When he saw her, well, I didn't know what to do really so I limped over to say hello."

Peter leaned in toward January as if he was telling her a secret.

"I was faking a sprained ankle because I didn't know how to dance." January laughed and smiled.

"When I got over there, I saw that she had her foot in a cast. What happened I asked her? I jumped off the porch and landed on a shovel handle. Just a stupid accident she said. It doesn't hurt but I got six weeks in this thing. Then she asked what happened to me. I told her my leg was asleep because I figured with her broken leg we wouldn't be dancing. Well that was a mistake. Great she said then we can still dance. Vroom off we went, probably danced every song until midnight."

He paused but January didn't say anything. She was afraid she would say the wrong thing.

"We bought a new car once, saved for I don't know something like two years and finally got the deal we wanted on the perfect car. I got to pick the car and she got to pick the color, Silver." Peter said then turned to January like an old friend.

"Not my idea of a good color but a deal is a deal and the car was a good deal too. I drove the old wagon, and she got the new car." Peter paused but January knew he wasn't finished with the story.

"Just about every day when I got home I would walk around the car. Beautiful coupe only new car I ever bought. I was going to make sure we took care of it. About the fourth day she came out and asked me what I was doing. Just checking the car I said, I want to make

sure we keep it up. Don't you trust me? She asked
   I said sure but it could get hit by someone when you're in the market or something. The next day I come home and the passenger door was covered with mud and some black stuff. What happened to the car? I asked her. Oh my, she said." Then Peter paused and looked at January as if he needed her to understand Mary before they meet.
   "Everything she said starts with 'Oh.' Oh Boy, Oh well, Oh my, Oh no. anyway she said, Oh my is something wrong? The next thing I know she brought me a bucket full of suds a sponge, and a big towel."
   Peter smiled. In his mind he could see his young wife holding a bucket of sudsy water clean towel thrown over her shoulder.
   "I went right out and washed off the door till it was sparkling." Peter said turning to look at January. "I looked and looked but I couldn't find anything wrong with the car. I don't know what you did I told her but there is nothing wrong with that door. Are you sure she asked then right away she said you're right and she didn't even look at the door." Peter smiled at January.
   "Better wash the whole car now. It looks funny with just one clean door." January felt the warmth in Peter's eyes it was enough to warm the coldest night.
   "She tricked me." Peter said looking at her as if he was pleading his case. "I said well why didn't you say something? Just like she said to me about being Jewish. I would always say that when she got Me.... Why didn't

you just say so. For the fifteen years we owned that car she would tell me, honey I think maybe somebody dinged the car at the market and that's how I knew it was time for me to wash the car. Just about every week except in winter. Honey, She would say, better check the car, could be a ding on it somewhere. We had fun, didn't matter what it was."

January saw a tear form in Peter's eye. She stood to get him a tissue but she looked a little too long. Her stomach cramped and she could feel a flood rushing toward her eyes. Quickly she jumped up and grabbed the box of tissue careful to make sure Peter could not see how his story affected her.

"Did you have any kids?" January asked quickly dabbing her eyes before turning back to Peter.

"We had a son." Taking a tissue that January offered as she turned. "We named him William. He died in a car wreck when he was eleven. I suppose she is with him now." A smile flowed into the deep lines on his face as just before tears raced south. He dried them talking through the tissue.

"After William died she would set the table for three. She would tell me his spirit may want to sit a bit and setting his place would let him know that we loved him on account of him being so young when he died." Peter swallowed and tossed the tissue into the trash. January could see the pain in his blank look. He looked worn in that moment and January realized for the first time that he was frail.

"I didn't know what to say, so I didn't say much." Peter said looking down. January understood that this pain was not from losing his son but from not knowing how to comfort his wife. She stared at him wondering if she could help such a deep and worn pain.

"Sorry." January said, wanting to touch his hand but resisting because her training told her not to.

"One day she helped the neighbor get her husband to the hospital." Peter said turning to looked at January

"It was a minor heart attack, he was okay. She came home late all in a rush trying to get dinner on the table before I got home. She always worried about dinner. She knew I would be hungry after work. Well, traffic was good that day and I had beaten her home so I got started on dinner. She rushed in and pretty much froze when she saw that I had set the table for three."

Nothing changed but January felt Peter was looking so deep into her eyes he was reading her feelings from the night before.

"I didn't set the place for Will, I set it for her. I saw her dry a tear with a kitchen towel and that was it. That was the last time we set the table for three."

January was touched by how much Peter loved his wife. She wished she could feel that way about Jeremy. "Did you ever have a fight?" She asked then immediately felt mortified because she remembered she was never supposed to bring up negative things about someone who had just died. She had allowed her personal problems to affect her work. She was supposed to be in control but damn Jeremy had invaded her safe space.

"Sure." Peter said comfortable leaning back in the chair.

"She had a fight with some folks at the Church, I don't remember what it was about but she decided she wanted to move. She spent a few weeks sitting around the house depressed wanted to move up to be near her sister. Great girl her sister Heather, anyway she asked a couple times and I said no. One day we were sitting at the breakfast table and she asked again. Something about it hit me wrong so I got gruff with her. I made it clear in no uncertain terms. I'm not quitting my job. I got 16 years in and I am not quitting.

We have vacation we can take to see your sister and that's plenty good enough. She didn't say anything, and that was her way. Everybody has their own way of dealing with things. Some folks explode, some cry, some well, they don't say anything. We sat there I don't know ten minutes maybe in dead silence. We didn't even eat just sat there. Finally she reached out with her small hand and grabbed the jar of honey picked it up and was looking at the label then she turned to me and said; clover honey is the best, isn't that what you always say? Yes, I like it best I told her and she started spreading it on her toast." January had not thought much about the story but Peter turned to her and she couldn't look away.

"I didn't know it then but I learned later. She had taken that moment to let it go. As important as it was, weeks of asking me and she just let it go." Peter turned stood and walked to his deceased wife. He took her hand and gave it three little kisses.

"Three kisses?" January asked.

"The dog had puppies." Peter said grinning at his wife." January didn't know what he was talking about.

Peter did not look at January. He stood staring at his wife holding her hand.

"The puppies were so cute she would pick them up and give them three kisses. Well look at that I told her, I never get three kisses and from that day on every night I got three kisses goodnight."

Peter turned to look at January with a smile as they both sat down.

"Our next trip to see her sister she told us her husband had cheated on her and she was moving back home. Oh my, good riddance Mary said waving her hand. I never liked him much anyway. Peter looked at January with a smile. She had never met anyone so full of simple joy. She felt he could see her pain and knew how to help her.

"Clover honey, that's how I knew. The more she did for me the more I wanted to do for her. We had a nice life."

There was silence for awhile. January knew she should say something profound but she was not in control. .January walked to her car after work glancing up to see a harder snowfall than when she started the shift. Without thinking much about it she decided to go to the market. "It feels nice to be out." She told herself, "I might as well stop for a few things." She made a mental list as she drove; Bread, always bread peanut butter and half and half for the coffee. She wasn't sure she needed it but better to have it than to run out. Cranking the stereo up she sang along with every song trying not to think much about what the temperature would be when she got home.

She stood in the aisle two feet from the peanut butter staring at the little golden bear. "A bear…figures." she muttered below her breath admitting to no-one that she had been "a bit" of a bear to live with. "I wonder if that's clover honey?" she thought.

Jeremy didn't say a word when she walked in. He had learned to protect himself by waiting for her to set the temperature. He was standing at the sink eating the last bite of peanut butter toast.

"Hi." He said not looking at her as he put the plate in the sink.

"Hi." She said flopping the bag on the counter glancing at the plate and his slow moving jaw. "I got you some honey." She said pulling the bear out of the bag and putting it on the counter next to him.

"Honey?" He asked mouth still half full of toast.

"Not just any honey, clover honey. That's the best kind." She gave him a small peck on the cheek and went to shower and change.

He stopped chewing when she showed him the honey bear. He was a little confused. He was expecting to get the cold shoulder and for her to still be angry. He watched her walk toward the bedroom as he chomped and swallowed. He looked down at the plate in the sink then picked it up and put it in the dishwasher.

The End

Made in the USA
Columbia, SC
16 September 2024